The Slum Sisters' Wish

EMMA HARDWICK

COPYRIGHT

Title: The Slum Sister's Wish

First published in 2021

ISBN: 9798477817344 (Print)

CONTENTS

The Prodigy	4
No Benefits to Love	12
The Beginning of the End	23
Friend and Traitor	36
Love, Power and Lies	55
The Announcement	76
Illegitimate	96
Marriage and Misery	120
The Journey	133
Elizabeth	155
Denial	175
Headline News	185
Never to Return	196
Drastic Actions	203
Justice	224
Help from an Unexpected Source	237
Missing	242
The Guilty and the Innocent	250
The Visitors	264

1

THE PRODIGY

Manchester, 1892

The bustling army of Salford Quays' workers battled against the bitter cold. Dense fog made the atmosphere worse, oppressive, claustrophobic even. The low cloud developed over the Irish Sea, and the icy wind drove it onshore toward the northwest coast of England, rendering the land invisible. Ships anchored where they lay, their captains unable to detect the faintest glow of a pilot light or the distant flash of a lighthouse. Hundreds of shipwrecks littered that stretch of coastline, a grim testament to men's foolishness and the treachery of the weather.

Dockside life was reduced to sinister shapeless phantoms that floated through the streets. The thick atmosphere absorbed sound, muting the noise of loading and unloading at the busy docks. Street and coach lamps were ineffective. Their meagre light only produced an opaque, yellow glow that bounced off the fog, rendering them useless.

Young Mary Errington sat in a small nook at the far side of a nearby office. Mr Porter had struggled to find a place where she could work comfortably. Although a towering structure, the busy warehouse was cramped. Every inch of floor space was covered with boxes. Eventually, Porter allocated her a small space under the staircase, the only place big enough to wedge a desk. Not a sophisticated piece of furniture, it was two trestles with a board across them.

The corner was dark, but Mary had a bright lamp on her desk, illuminating the numerals she carefully wrote into the giant ledger. Oblivious to all the noise around her, she meticulously entered the correct number into the correct column. Then she totted up all the figures and wrote the total at the bottom of the ivory-coloured page. Instinctively, Mary knew that she had added it all up correctly but checked herself anyway. The idea of someone finding fault with her work caused her great anxiety since she would never live down the shame of being wrong.

Edgar Porter watched the girl in awe. It was pure chance that he had found Mary Errington, and he was happy that he had. Taking up a recommendation to him by a ragged school teacher in Angel Meadows, she was well worth the investment.

"Edgar, the child is a prodigy," exclaimed Bess Harrington.

Bess had been sent to the chandlers on an errand to order goods for her merchant seaman husband.

"Numbers!" exclaimed Bess. "This girl can add up a row of numbers in a flash. It baffles me. I can't tell you how she does it. I couldn't do it in a month of Sundays."

Edgar smiled. Bess was prone to exaggeration.

"Now, now, Bess. How old is this prodigy then?"

"Sixteen."

"That's a bit old to still be at school. Most girls from these parts are out working in the factories at ten years old."

"She is helping me teach the others. I can never grasp the true story, Edgar. Mary looks after herself very well. She works for free at the ragged school. We can't afford to pay her, and she never asks for anything. Yet, her big sister, Anna, is labouring down at the Portuguese greengrocer on Malvern Street. She's worked for Mr Perreira since she was twelve. Like I say, it's a funny business. But all beside the point, my dear Edgar. You have to meet the girl."

"It is an unusual story, Bess," Edgar added with a laugh. "Perhaps I should employ this genius."

It was just what Bess was hoping to hear.

> "I can send her over if you like?" she said eagerly.

Feeling railroaded by the enthusiastic woman, Edgar wished that he had never suggested the idea and lamented shooting off his mouth without thinking yet again. Bess stared at him until she got the answer she wanted.

> "Alright, Bess. I can't promise you anything, but it will be interesting to see what this prodigy is capable of."

> "Thank you, Edgar." she cheered, clapping her chubby hands together. "Bless your soul. You know that I would never lie to you, and I won't hold you to anything. I promise you won't be disappointed."

Edgar recalled his first meeting with Mary on a crisp Tuesday morning when the sullen young woman presented herself at his office. She had an air of confidence seldom displayed by someone of her class or age. She held herself erect, and when he put out his hand to greet her, she shook it firmly. Edgar got the impression that she could have made a fine general if she had been born a male in a privileged family. Mary not only had confidence but also an arrogance that warned him never to underestimate her. She may have been born into a working-class family, but she was adamant that she would not die in one.

Even before Edgar Porter offered the girl a seat, he knew that he would employ her.

"Good morning, Miss Errington." he greeted formally.

"Mr Porter," the girl said with a polite nod.

Edgar noted that she had not referred to him as sir. It didn't annoy him. He interpreted her response as a young lady refusing to be intimidated by class or gender. He got straight to the point.

"Porter and Porter Chandlery is long-established. My father opened the business seventy years ago, and we have built a fine reputation over the decades. As you are aware, we provide goods to ships in the harbour. Thus, we must ensure that our stores are suitably always stocked. We have a vast warehouse with goods coming and going all the time. It can get rather complicated managing the goods inwards—and out," he explained in a business-like manner.

"I understand."

"I have many accountants and clerks working here, given the amount of work involved. All of them are male. To be honest, Mary, I have never employed a woman in such a responsible position. Your appointment as the first of the fairer sex working here will certainly cause a furore."

Edgar studied Mary carefully. He couldn't see a hint of resentment or worry on her face.

> "I can work faster and more accurately than any man in your employ," Mary announced clinically.

Edgar was taken aback by her reply, but he didn't react. He gave her a stern instruction.

> "Your teacher says that you excel with numbers. So, I have prepared a test for you. Here is a column. Add it up and give me a total. Using mental arithmetic alone.

Mary picked up the sheet of paper. There were fifty numbers to tot up. She didn't flinch. Edgar watched her eyes lock on each number as they travelled down the length of the column.

> "Five hundred and eighty-seven pounds and twenty-six and a half pence."
>
> "Do you want to double-check that?" asked Edgar.
>
> "No, Sir. It is correct."

Edgar knew that it was. He had added the numbers before the meeting, but whereas it had taken Mary all of thirty seconds, it had taken him five minutes, with a pen and paper.

> "I will appoint you as a junior clerk. You will report to Mr Godwin. He is strict but fair."

Mary nodded.

"Can you start tomorrow?"

"Yes, Mr Porter."

"Is there anything you need to complete at school?"

"No, Mr Porter."

Edgar nodded.

"Mr Porter, I need to be frank."

"Carry on."

"I appreciate this opportunity, but I won't be working here forever."

Edgar frowned. He was surprised by her boldness, but he found her candour refreshing.

"I have plans to study further. University."

"That is an ambitious plan for a young woman. Are you sure that you are capable of being accepted? Not many women are?"

Edgar waited to see if the statement would rile her.

"Yes, I am capable, and yes, I will be accepted."

Edgar raised his eyebrows.

"You will be here at seven o'clock tomorrow morning, Miss Errington."

"Thank you, Mr Porter."

Mary shook her new employer's hand. As he led her out of the office, he noted that she had not smiled during the interview. Mary had not shown fear or humour. She showed no trace of joy at her appointment. In fact, Mary Errington had shown no emotion at all.

2

NO BENEFITS TO LOVE

It was eight o'clock in the evening when Mary finally put down her pen. She had checked and rechecked her work. Eventually, she was satisfied that it was perfect. Mary was always the last person to leave the office every night, except for Mr Porter. Everyone knew that Edgar Porter had a wife and four sons, but whether he ever went home to them was a mystery. The office was empty except for a young boy washing the floor, but the great warehouse below was still hustling and bustling with the night shift. The docks never slept. There was always a ship to be loaded by the morning.

Mary's hair was scraped back off her face and twisted into a severe knot at the nape of her neck. She was plain, yet nobody forgot her after they saw her. With a hooked nose and thin lips that looked like a gash across her face, she never smiled. Her eyes were tiny bright blue beads that were barely noticeable. Her constant frown forced her hooded eyelids into narrow slits. The habit of moving her head abruptly, with eyes wide open, seldom blinking, made her look like a bird of prey. Her mannerisms were intimidating, making those who encountered her imagine a hawk about to rip its prey to shreds.

Mary put on her long coat, made from a fine quality wool and long enough to reach her ankles. Next, she put on her hat and scarf, picked up her umbrella and made for the door. Looking very smart as she walked through the warehouse, no one shouted out goodbyes or made any jokes with her as she passed by. The men had quickly learned that Mary was not approachable like the other young warehouse women they worked with. After suffering her cold stare and aloof personality, the chaps soon gave up any attempt at banter and decided to ignore her.

"Bloody strange one that." Berty Higgins said to his friend as he watched Mary walk by.

"She's a young 'un. Maybe she's just shy, mate."

"Bloody stuck up, me thinks," said Berty.

"She lives down the street from me aunt," said Jack Murphy.

"Where's that then?" asked Berty.

"The Meadows," answered Jack.

"The Meadows! How does a lass from the slums dress like she is from the bright side of the street?"

"She lives on Angel Street, but don't ask me more, Berty. I just know what me Ma tells me."

"So hoity-toity. Ideas above her station, alright," complained Berty.

"That's enough now, lad. You're like a bloody dripping tap. Have you taken a liking to the girl then, Berty?"

He punched Jack roughly on the arm.

"No chance of that, mate. I'm just saying."

But Jack had lost interest in teasing his colleague. He had to load freight and had no time to gossip about Mary Errington.

Mary left the dockyard, head held high. When she was out of sight of her colleagues, she whipped into a shadowy dark alley where she would be invisible. She exchanged her good boots for the old ones that she kept in her carpetbag. Mary was determined to be clean and well-dressed wherever she went, but she didn't want to ruin her good boots walking home. In the dark, nobody would see her scuffed old shoes. Irrespective of the exchange, Mary knew that the old things were on her feet, and she felt embarrassed.

The young girl had never known life beyond Salford, yet she felt deeply ashamed of her surroundings. Locals who watched her pass by were perplexed by the girl's surliness. This night there were no stares, no judgement. Mary was anonymous in the fog. She imagined a different life and practised ignoring the savage poverty around her.

Cocooned by the white cloud, Mary saw herself in a different world. She seldom allowed herself to dream, but tonight she did. She was walking down a broad tree-lined boulevard, the 'The Mall' in London. She could see the lights of Buckingham Palace in the distance. Dressed in fine clothes, she was carrying a polished black leather satchel. She walked along Park Lane. A hotel doorman hailed a cab for her, and she gave the driver a well-to-do address in Kensington. The cab trundled past clubs, five-star hotels, and expensive shops, past parkland with soaring trees, landscaped ponds and marble fountains decorated with cherubs and harps. She imagined that it was a balmy night, and people were out walking. As she left the cab, she could hear someone playing the piano when she passed a restaurant. Next door, beautiful harmonies from a string quartet floated onto the pavement.

Mary was jolted back to reality as a wagon turned into the narrow street. The driver didn't see her, and she scrambled to push herself against a filthy wall and allow it to pass. The cart stank of rotting carcasses collected from the shambles.

She deliberately turned into Churchill Street. The choice would take her out of her way, but it was worth it. She reached an unobtrusive door which was squashed between a laundry and a tobacconist. A small, tarnished plaque above the letterbox read: *Alec Riddle, Solicitor*. Mary pushed open the door with a knot of anxiety in her stomach. She savoured it. Mostly, she was devoid of emotion, but fear had the power to excite her.

She climbed the staircase to the second floor, then Mary approached a door and knocked discreetly. A few seconds later, it was opened by a man at least fifteen years her senior.

"I was wondering if I would see you tonight," said Riddle.

"I worked late."

The older man showed her into the small flat, which also doubled as his office. The first room functioned as his office. It was neat, with a bookcase that extended to the ceiling, housing volumes of leather-bound law books. He closed the door to his office and stepped into the other room, which doubled as a bed-sit. The small kitchen was immaculate. A table with two chairs stood next to the fire, and there was an armchair in the corner. Alec pushed aside a curtain to reveal a large comfortable bed pushed up against the wall. It was dressed in clean cotton sheets and a thick eiderdown. Alec delighted in his clean apartment. It made him proud. In his mind, it was a hygienic pinprick in a sea of filth, and Mary was the perfect, pure, innocent young woman he chose to share it with.

Alec Riddle looked down at the young girl. They had been meeting secretly since she was fourteen. He had met her at the tobacconist downstairs, where she was buying a box of matches. The shop was busy. When Mary went to pay, she bumped into someone and dropped the penny she was holding. As it rolled away, she sunk to her knees, then tried to coax the coin out from under the heavy wooden counter. The other customers were becoming impatient while they waited for the young girl to get on with the transaction. Most of them were bad-natured and heckled her.

Mary's face was red from anger and humiliation. *'How dare these low-born folk harass me?'*

She hoped to catch a glimpse of the faces that scorned her. She would remember each one of them, and one day, if the opportunity arose, she would make them pay for writing her off.

Alec Riddle stood behind Mary in the queue. As he watched her, he noted her discomfort. Then, he pushed towards her, bent down, and helped the girl to her feet.

"Here, lass, we can fish the penny out later," he said kindly.

Mary felt Alec push a coin into her hand.

"Take it now. Buy what you need to."

"Thank you," she replied, face blood red, unable to meet his gaze.

Mary bought the matches and left the errant penny under the counter for later, then turned and pushed her way through the mean crowd. Alec bought what he needed. As he stepped out of the tobacconist shop, he found Mary waiting for him outside. Alec raised an eyebrow and looked at her questioningly.

"I don't know how to repay you. My mum lives quite a distance from here. It'll take me a while to get to her and bring a penny back—" she lied, ashamed of her Angel Meadow address.

"It's no bother."

The attractive early thirties man smiled down at her, seeming charming but reserved. His good accent told her he was educated.

"My name is Alec Riddle. That's my sign next to the door."

"Mary Errington."

"How old are you?"

"Sixteen," she lied.

"Come and have a cup of tea with me."

Alec's demeanour was neither lecherous nor intimidating. Mary turned to face the man, her flitting eyes assessing him like a falcon.

"Go on. Come on up," he said, nodding toward the door.

"Are you going to hurt me?" she asked directly.

Her question took him off guard. His face softened.

"No! Nothing of the sort! You simply look weary, and it's cold. I was glad that I could help you earlier. You said it's a long way, and your coat is a bit threadbare. I thought some tea would warm you up, that's all," he said kindly.

Mary was not afraid of him but remained alert after learning to read people at a young age. Her intuition told her that Alec Riddle was likely an opportunist but not a predator. That suited her well. Mary was also an opportunist, and Alec had prickled her interest from the moment she discovered he was a solicitor. She took a few paces towards him then murmured:

"Alright, I will come up for tea."

"Right then," he said, smiling as he opened the door.

"What if the neighbours see me?"

"My neighbour, Mrs Sturges, is half-blind and as deaf as a doorpost," he laughed.

Mary didn't laugh. She didn't even smile. She did wonder if he might take a romantic interest in her. How her mind arrived at the question was a mystery, but it gave her an idea. She had a tiny window of opportunity to contemplate a relationship with Alec Riddle.

She was an inexperienced virgin, but she would allow him to seduce her. Within the moments it took to climb the flight of stairs to his office, Mary had evaluated the situation fully and mastered her plan. If she approached the idea with an open mind, it could become lucrative. If Alec Riddle attempted to seduce her, she would cooperate. She would do it in the hope that he would pay her. It was a gamble. This was the only time in her life that Mary would take a chance and risk failure. Mary didn't think of it as prostitution but a partnership. If there was no reward, she would simply never see him again.

Alec Riddle was not a monster. He approached Mary intellectually, giving her a choice. This appealed to Mary's unsentimental personality. He undressed himself, then he undressed Mary. She had just blossomed into womanhood, and he took pleasure in arousing her. Mary felt neither happy nor sad, only a deep pulsating pleasure, which was the closest she had ever come to feeling satisfied. Alec was thrilled at finding a virgin. She was clean, and there was no fear of disease. Pregnancy was a great concern—he would be careful. Riddle knew that he had baptised Mary into the world of sensuality, and he didn't want to share the girl with anyone else. He was willing to support her if she promised him the exclusivity of her lovely body. But there were no guarantees of her loyalty. It was Alec's turn to take a risk.

Afterwards, Alec washed her tenderly. It had been a painful experience for the girl, but she didn't flinch as he wiped the blood from her thighs.

"Will you come to me whenever you can?" he asked with a smile.

Mary nodded.

"If I find out that you have been with another man, we will terminate this contract forthwith."

Mary understood. They spoke the same language.

"What if you fall in love with a boy? What will you do?"

"I have no intention of falling in love."

"Love is tricky," he confided. "It can creep up on you."

"There is no benefit to falling in love, Mr Riddle."

Mary was telling the truth. She had watched people lie, cheat and murder in the name of love. Love was a destructive distraction. She had met many people who professed to be in love, but none of them were happy with each other.

When she reached the door, Alec's finger pushed a small object into her loosely clenched fist. She refused to look desperate and buried the thing in the palm of her hand until she reached the street. It was a note folded into the tiniest block. Mary unravelled it and gasped. It was the most money that she had ever seen. She nodded her head in self-congratulation. The risk had paid off. It would be a beautiful partnership, so much so she even managed a small smile to celebrate her success.

Mary put the money into her dress pocket. She was excited. Money was power, and this was her first step to freedom.

3

THE BEGINNING OF THE END

Mary arrived home much later than usual.

> "Where in God's name have you been?" Jeanie Errington grizzled through her teeth. "You've had me waiting and waiting. I thought someone had cracked yer head open."

Jeanie held a chipped glass in her hand and was swaying from side to side. In between sentences, the drunken woman stopped to take a sip of gin. She was used to Mary getting home late, but it was the first time that the girl had arrived home that late. Jeanie was not concerned about Mary's safety. She was concerned that Mary would get robbed for her wages. If the girl's pay packet was stolen, Ma Errington would not be able to buy her next bottle of gin.

"I've been working," shrugged Mary.

"I have a good mind to go down to your boss man and set him straight on a few things. It's dangerous for a young lass like you to be about the streets at this time of the morning." Jeanie whined.

It was an empty threat. Mary knew that her mother would never go down to the quays and speak to Mr Porter.

"It's always dangerous, Ma, even on the brightest Sunday morning."

"What is that man thinking by keeping you at work so late? I wish you would get a decent job. Your sister works decent hours. Mr Perreira sends her home at eight o'clock, and she gets time off on a Sunday. They are Catholics, you know, they refuse to work on the Lord's Day."

"I have a decent job too."

Mary regretted rising to the bait as she watched Jeanie pull up her nose and scowl.

"Stop interfering in my business. Stick your big fat beak into Anna's life if you want to be a fusspot," Mary pouted.

"Your sister knows how to manage herself."

Mary tried her best to ignore her mother. It had been a long day, and all she wanted to do was wash, count her money, and go to sleep.

"What good is this job of yours? You hardly give me anything. The other girls in the row hand are earning far more than you."

Jeanie was becoming nasty.

"Then Anna should take a second job. Where is she now?"

"Anna works hard for Mr Perreira. She is entitled to some fun at night," said Jeanie in a tired drawl. "I have told you before, sweetheart. There are a lot of wealthy men about if you go to the right places. Anna likes going to the St George's Club at the quays."

"First time I've heard of a Men's Club allowing ladies," Mary countered.

"Well, Miss Know-It-All, Anna is mixing with the toffs down there, so she is."

"It's a dive of a pub, hiding behind a fancy name, filled with working men pretending to be important."

"She wants to find a husband, and she will. I feel it in my bones."

"What about Mario?"

> "That won't last very long. Besides, they are Catholic, and we are not."

Mary shook her head. If she had a sense of humour, she would have laughed loudly.

> "Anna knows all the blokes, and she's a good-looking lass, our Anna is."

Mary ignored her mother and poured hot water into an enamel bowl. She lathered her hands with carbolic soap and began to wash her hands and face.

> "She may not have a penny to her name right now, but one day she will catch a wealthy bloke, and he will look after all of us," said Jeanie.

The mother's eyes had a dreamy look about them. Clearly, she was imagining the luxurious world that her son-in-law would bankroll for her.

Mary watched her mother sitting by the range. She had her elbow propped on the table, and the cracked glass was dangling precariously from her hand. With a ciggie hanging out of the side of her mouth, she would puff at it now and again. Mary had heard her mother's laments so many times that she could repeat them in her sleep.

> "Anna should not be near those men. They will take advantage of her."

"What do you know about that?" Jeanie chuckled.

Jeanie's false laugh riled Mary, which encouraged her to lash out in retaliation to her mother's snide remark.

"And it's stupid of my sister to give you everything that she earns."

Mary knew that Jeanie got angry at the thought of Anna withholding money from her, and Mary made sure to rub it in every time that Jeanie being vicious.

"You are an ungrateful little wench. We would all live better if you weren't so selfish."

"I pay my rent every week, Ma. You won't get a penny more out of me."

Jeanie stared at her second child and wondered where she had gone wrong in raising her. Anna would do anything for Jeanie, but this here Mary, she was a different kettle of fish. She had a mean, cruel streak in her. Mary also kept her cards close to her chest—one hand never knew what the other was doing.

Mary stared down at her mother. She felt no empathy for the pathetic woman, only disgust. Jeanie was one of those meek, weak, accepting souls who was satisfied to wait until she could collect on someone else's luck.

"I've put my rent in the tin," Mary said, pointing at the rusty old caddy.

"It's time to raise the rent. You can ye give me a little extra this week. I need to get out of this row for a few hours. I want to have a pint or two at The Dragon tonight. A little entertainment will make me feel much better. Anna and Sybil are coming with me."

"No."

"I will whip your bad manners right out of you, girl," shouted Jeanie.

"Go on, Ma. I am waiting," taunted Mary, knowing full well that her mother had neither the drive nor the energy to beat her. It was an empty threat that she had used on her daughters since they were tiny.

"You don't love me as much as your sister does. Anna would walk over hot coals for me," sobbed Jeanie.

"For once, you are actually right about something. I wouldn't walk over hot coals for you," Mary sneered down at her mother. *'And I don't bloody love you at all.'*

Mary went into the room where they all slept. She closed the door behind her and began to undress. She was glad she sewed a secret pocket into her dress. It was perfect for hiding her weekly wages. It served two purposes: a robber on the street would never find her cash, and nor would her mother.

She carefully extracted her money for the week along with the extra she earned from Riddle that night. Pulling a piece of loose skirting away from the wall revealed a narrow hole. She put her hand in then bent her arm at an odd angle to reach the small black tin that secured her wealth. She deftly slid it out from its hiding place. It was becoming heavy. *A good sign.* The feel of the secret cache in her hand pleased her clinical brain, and she smiled broadly in the dark. She put her earnings into the tin, then made sure that the lid was screwed on tightly. The last thing she wanted was the rats nibbling the pound notes. She popped it back, replaced the skirting, and relaxed. It had been a long day and eventful day, and she reflected on her success once more. Finally, she hung her clothes on a rusty nail that had been hammered into the decaying wall for that very purpose. Then she lay down on the worn mattress and fell into a deep, dreamless sleep.

Mary woke up just before five o'clock. Although she had only a few hours' sleep, she felt fresh and alert. She had to be at Porter and Porter by seven. She looked forward to going to work. It was engrossing, requiring her full attention. This enabled her to ignore her woeful surroundings at home and escape the misery of The Meadows. She made a cup of tea and washed her hands again. She was fastidious about personal hygiene. She rubbed charcoal on her teeth, thoroughly coating every inch of her mouth, then rinsed it off, ensuring that not a shred of the black stain remained. She treated herself to a peppermint, her only indulgence for the week. She brushed her hair and scraped it off her face, then she twisted it severely and rolled it into a knot that would last the whole day. She would be neat, clean, and sitting at her desk by seven o'clock.

Mary Errington stepped out of the front door. She looked at odds with her environment. She was a well-groomed girl in a sea of poverty. Walking down her street, she was heckled for being clean and smart. The neighbourhood scallies loved to think they were humiliating her, but they were wrong. She felt no shame in her own skin, just a calm hatred for them. She had been raised in the squalor of Angel Meadows, but she had no empathy for the wretches that littered the pavements around her. There was no commonality from Mary's perspective. Charity was the church's responsibility, not hers. There was enough money in the mighty empire to house every pauper in a palace, and she would not do the establishment's job for it. She had read a pamphlet by a German man purporting to have an economic theory that would alleviate poverty and uplift the working class. The man's name was Karl Marx. He had written the pamphlet in conjunction with someone else. For the life of her, she couldn't remember the other chap's name. That's how insignificant he was. Their ideas had not impressed her. She had no intention of sharing anything that she earned. When she got her hands of a copy of their pamphlet, she serenely tore it to pieces and threw it away.

Mary was a long down the street when she saw two figures walking toward her. Although they were far off, Anna's giggle was unmistakable. The man she was with was propping her up, and it was obvious that the evening had not yet ended for them.

"Oi! Mary!" shouted Anna, clearly drunk. "Where're you going? It's still the middle of the night."

Mary didn't answer. Her drunk sister's question didn't merit a sober reply. Anna grabbed Mary's arm as she passed by.

"Here! Here! Mary, look!" she called out in a stage whisper. "This is Mario Perreira."

She pointed to the young man with her thumb.

"We have had a smashing evening, so we have."

Mary recognised Mario. He was the son of Anna's boss, Mr Perreira. The Perreiras were a staunch, Portuguese, Catholic tribe who had settled in Cheetham where they would create their fortune. Mary found it commendable that the Perreira family worked so hard. Each member of the family, including the children, had responsibilities. There were sisters, brothers, cousins, nephews, nieces, and every remote family member they could fit either crewed on a ship or worked in the store. Anna was very lucky to be employed by them. It was a steady job. At a certain age, Mr Perreira would return to Portugal and live a good life next to the ocean. The business in Cheetham would then be passed to the next generation, and so the cycle would continue with the hardworking immigrants ensuring that one generation would support the last.

> "Is not he terribly handsome?" whispered Anna while Mario hovered in the background.

Mary looked from her vivacious sister to Mario. Anna was still wearing the same clothes that she had worked in the previous day, and her hair was a mess. Mario was trying to appear aloof but was not convincing. He had his hands in his pockets and was leaning against a sooty red brick wall. He had a smile on his lips. From the corner of his eye, he was studying the interaction between the two young women. The siblings couldn't have been more different. Mary had harsh angular features, but Anna was a curvaceous, sensual beauty. Her perfect complexion was enhanced with large eyes and long, pitch-black eyelashes. She radiated joy and good humour. Her sensuous mouth was quick to smile, and her hair was a wild mass of tresses that she struggled to keep under a hat. When she undressed in front of Mario, her loose curls tumbled down her perfect back, and contrasted with her smooth, pale skin. Mario couldn't contain himself, and he spent many evenings indulging himself by exploiting her. He told how much he enjoyed her passion, her beauty, her body and that he loved her. Mario didn't dare tell Anna that he had no intention of marrying her.

Mario was the crown prince of the Perreira family. Everything had worked in his favour in that he was the eldest child and spoilt to death. From a young age, his mother made it clear that *'only a Portuguese girl would be good enough to marry'*. There had to be significant courtship supervised by the mothers, aunts, and cousins. The pair would get married in a church. His bride was guaranteed to be a virgin, and if she was not, the marriage would be annulled, with her husband being the only witness. The bride would wear her mother's wedding dress. It had to have a long silk train embroidered with flowers. This showy status symbol was guaranteed to impress the aunts and grandmothers. The church would be a mass of flowers and candles while the happy couple knelt on red velvet cushions adorned with gold trim. The great marble altar would dwarf them. The priest would offer them the sacrament. They would say their vows, promising to forsake all others, and they would be declared man and wife. In order of importance: Mama Perreira, the Pope, the Virgin and God would all be relieved that the couple were hitched and not living in sin. If Mario impregnated his beloved within a few months, nobody would complain if he spent his free time with a mistress.

"He really loves me," Anna giggled. "He is teaching me Portuguese so that I can understand his family."

"You're making a mistake, Anna."

Anna felt annoyed by the remark. Mary was always putting her down. Her sister was miserable, and she took it out upon everyone around her. Anna walked over to Mario and took his arm. She pushed her body up against him seductively.

"One day, you will know happiness," Anna said to her sister.

She looked up at Mario, unable to keep her adoration of him a secret.

"We need to hurry, Mario. We need to be at work within the hour," she giggled.

Mario looked down at Anna and crushed her against his chest. He took Anna's face in his hands, closed his eyes, and kissed her passionately with an open mouth. He wanted to embarrass the young, disapproving Mary.

Mary didn't have time to waste on Anna and her boyfriend. She had her list of priorities for the day. The first one was Porter and Porter, the second was Alec Riddle.

Mario couldn't wait to see the look on Mary's face as he ravished Anna. He opened his eyes to see if Mary was watching him, but she was gone.

'Vadia Feia', he whispered under his breath. Foolishly, Anna took the phrase to be another of Mario's smooth-talking compliments for her ears only, completely misunderstanding its true meaning: an expletive-laden criticism of her sister's looks.

4

FRIEND AND TRAITOR

Dicky Woods pulled his flat cap low over his eyes as he walked toward Jeanie's cramped back-to-back house, trying his best to blend into the crowd. When he reached Jeanie's, he bounced up the steps to the front entrance. Instead of opening the door immediately, first, he glanced around to see if anybody was watching him. It was a fatal mistake. Mavis McCrae identified him immediately. The last thing Dicky Woods needed was for Bernard Errington to find out that he was calling on his wife when he was working away from home. Dicky and Jeanie had been having a good carry-on for some time. It all started one night when he saw her at The Dragon. It was easy to get her attention—she was lonely. At first, they had just gone into the alley behind The Dragon and got on with it. Dicky was happy with the arrangement behind the pub, but Jeanie whined that it was too cold. Dicky was a confirmed bachelor who still lived with his mother in a small room down near the docks. Stupidly, Jeanie took him home, and within a few days, everybody knew that Dicky was servicing Bernie Errington's wife.

Dicky Woods was a small, vindictive man who quickly convinced Jeanie that he was her saviour. Lonely old Jeanie was desperate, gullible, and believed everything that Dicky told her. Soon, she was without friends and totally reliant on the spiteful, bitter fellow she had to support. Dicky was all talk, and he had grand plans. Every time Dicky had an idea, Jeanie would finance him out of the money that her husband earned. The situation was disgraceful. The closest Dicky came to working was a job at the local coffin house as a cleaner.

Bernard Errington was a mild man. He had lived on the sea for more years than he had lived on land. The sea had been his saviour. He headed to the Salford Quays when he was just thirteen, desperate to escape his cruel stepmother.

Bernard's mother had died from cholera when he was five, which left him an only child. His father, Steven Errington, adored the boy, but when he remarried, the new woman in his life was bitter, jealous of his relationship with the boy. Colleen Errington had a vicious temper and took the whip to him whenever she could.

> "I am sorry, son, that I ever let that witch into our lives," Steven would lament.

On an icy winter's afternoon, while Steven worked to support the fractured family, Colleen Errington had beaten Bernard so badly that he collapsed in a bloody heap on the cinder steps outside the house. Sally Cremer, a neighbour, had watched the scene and screamed for her husband to intervene. It took all Stewart Cremer's strength to pull Colleen off the lad. Everyone said she would have surely killed the boy if no one had intervened.

That night Steven Errington got home from his job at the cotton mill.

> "The brat is next door," screamed the maniacal Colleen.

Steven knocked on the Cremer's door, and Stewart opened it.

> "He's in a bad way, Steve. Your missis would have killed him."

Sally was not as polite and put him firmly in the picture.

> "You better get that lad away from that rabid feckin' shrew. You'll be shocked when you see the state of him. He won't be out of that bed for a week."

The two of them negotiated the narrow stairs and then to a cubby-hole of a room under the eaves. Steven stared down at his sickly child, his little body one big, bloody bruised pulp. The sight of his son's wounds stung his throat and his eyes. He blinked hard for a minute or so, then gave in and began to cry. Gently, he stroked his lad's hair. When he was confident the croak would be gone from his voice, Steven thanked his neighbours and went home.

He'd hardly opened the kitchen door, then Colleen screamed at him.

"Did year see yer little runt then?"

For a moment, Steven couldn't breathe. His surroundings seemed unfamiliar, and he couldn't hear anything. All he could see was the distorted face of a madwoman screaming at him, but the words themselves had no effect. He had sunk too far into a rage to care. Hitting her like he would have hit a man, she fell backwards, banging her head against the leg of the table. When she stood up, blood flowed from her nose and mouth, and she continued to scream. Of everything that she said, the only word he could identify was *'hate'*. She charged at him again, but this time he did a fine job of it. He put every ounce of fury behind his fist. Colleen lifted off the ground for a few seconds, then she flew backwards and landed on the floor unconscious.

Steven sank down onto a chair. He sat there for some time and slowly started to come to his senses. He looked about him. Everything came into focus. He saw a crisp image of his wife lying sparko on the floor. Suddenly, the light was too bright, like when he opened the front door on a summer day. It was as if he was waking up. Steven Errington realised that for a short while, he had lost his mind. Instead of feeling triumphant, he was ashamed.

Over the weeks, Bernard healed. One evening Steven sat his son down next to him.

"Colleen's gone," said Steven.

Bernard nodded.

"You didn't have to send her away for my sake. I want you to be happy, Da."

"She is not here anymore, and I am happy."

Bernard swallowed hard.

"Son, this place is a hole. You need to see the world."

Bernard looked at him with big eyes.

"Do you remember that book Sally Cremer read to us when you were still a young lad? It was called Robinson Crusoe."

Bernard's face lit up.

"Yes, I do remember it. It was a corker of a story. I loved it."

"You need an adventure, Bernard."

"I don't want to be eaten by a cannibal, Da."

"I am certain you won't," laughed Steven.

"Pack your bag tonight. Sally will write a note to Captain Masterton. The ship's name is *'The Destiny'*. I saved Captain Masterton's life in the Crimea. He will look after you."

The sea didn't make Bernard a tough old sea dog. Rather it gave him peace. Bernard was a good sailor. He gained a fine reputation as a mate and was sought by many captains to help sail his vessel through troubled waters.

He earned a good wage, and Jeanie would go down to the quay once a month and collect his earnings. His wife and children should have had a far better standard of living than they did, and he could never understand what all money was used for. There was nothing to show for it. The cupboards were empty, the house was dirty, and there was no furniture. He loathed to demand answers from Jeanie. She was fragile, and he didn't enjoy upsetting her. Angel Meadows was an incarnation of hell. He decided to take the matter in hand on his next shore leave and insist that Jeanie and the girls move to the countryside.

Bernard was in his mid-twenties when he had met Jeanie. His ship was in the dry cock of a Liverpool shipyard, and he was granted shore leave of a month. He booked into a small hotel near Church Street. The establishment was clean, and Bernard was looking forward to a month of luxury. He had no real expenses to cover, and his savings entitled him to fine lodgings.

A clean-living young man, he had no compulsion to frequent any brothels or drinking holes in the vicinity, so he collapsed onto the luxurious bed in his room, thinking of what to do to keep himself busy. He opened the French doors and stepped onto a small, tiled balcony, bound by a cast-iron railing, giving him a splendid view of Church Street. It was still early afternoon, and the weather was unusually balmy. Bernard decided to take a walk and perhaps stop somewhere and have a drink. It was a shame to be indoors on such a fine day.

He ambled down Church Street until he reached the corner where it joined Lord Street. Carefully crossing the junction, he studied everything around him. It had been a long time since he visited a city of this size, and it would pay to keep his wits about him. By three o'clock, he was ravenous. Spotting a tearoom on the opposite side of the street, he made his way toward it. After dodging a few carts and sidestepping out of the path of an oncoming omnibus, Bernard made a conscious decision to find his land legs as soon as possible—or he risked being fatally mowed down by something on wheels.

Reaching the tearoom shaken but alive, he put out his arm to open the door, but instead, it swung open from the inside, revealing a beautiful but dishevelled woman. Her eyes were bright blue, and her skin was pale. Her bonnet served no purpose, sitting on a bird's nest of unruly hair.

"Hello," he mumbled, so surprised that he couldn't manage much more.

"Well, are you coming in or aren't ya?" she asked with a broad country accent.

"May I?"

"Yes, of course. Let me find you a chair."

"Do you work here?" asked Bernard.

"No, but I gave you such a fright. It's only fair to find you a table to sit at."

Bernard smiled at her kindness.

"It has been a terrible day. I came here looking for a job, but the owner has gone out," she complained.

"May I buy you a cup of tea and something to eat while you wait for him to arrive? You will feel better."

Jeanie blushed.

"I'm sorry. I can't do that."

"Is somebody expecting you?"

"No, no, but I don't know you, so I can't be seen with a strange man if I want a job here," she stuttered.

"Well, let's find another tearoom, shall we? You will be anonymous. We will allow them to assume that we are married," Bernard said with a mischievous twinkle in his eye.

Jeanie's eyes widened.

"Oh! All right then. Thank you."

They walked all the way up towards Lime Street without speaking.

"Is this far enough?" Bernard asked her.

"Yes," She confirmed with a smile. "Nobody knows me on this side. This will do just fine."

Bernard married Jeanie six months later. Jeanie was older than Bernard by five years, but it was not that noticeable, and he didn't care. Jeanie was looking for someone to take care of her, and she was satisfied to marry a handsome man, in a smart uniform, who loved her.

Jeanie was still a virgin, and her introduction to carnal pleasures unleashed a monster that would leave her hungry for physical interaction for the rest of her life. Bernard spent a week with his young bride, then returned to sea. It was this monster that would ultimately destroy her family.

Bernard Errington was surprised to learn that Jeanie, one of eleven children, came from a wealthy background. Jeanie's father was a successful farmer in York, and they all worked with him. The family was ambitious, and they succeeded in creating one of the most productive pieces of land in England. John and Betsy Harrison were proud of their children, who all survived into adulthood. They had a growing tribe of grandchildren, and there were no feuds. They hoped that within a few generations, their legacy would be accepted into the finest schools that England could offer.

The only child who caused them concern was Jeanie, who was still unmarried and nearing thirty years old. In desperation, John and Betsy agreed that she should be sent to Liverpool to find work and hopefully a husband. Jeanie had an odd temperament that didn't endear people to her. She was pleasing to the eye and kind at heart, yet there was a melancholy that gripped her, creating the impression that she was fragile and no farmer was looking for a brittle wife.

Bernard never got the opportunity to meet his father-in-law. As Jeanie squandered more and more of Bernard's money, she was forced to find a cheaper place to live. Every time that Bernard came home, Jeanie was living in more squalor. Ultimately, her life spiralled out of control while Bernard was not there to manage the coffers. It was this descent into poverty that landed Jeanie in Angel Street and lost to her family.

Bernard was desperate. He needed somebody to watch over his wife while he was away. He decided that she would be better off in a boarding house than alone. This was the most disastrous decision the desperate husband ever made. The boarding house was in Matthew Street, owned by Mrs Woods, and Dicky Woods was her nephew.

Dicky Woods spent a lot of time with Jeanie, under the premise of 'looking after' her. Dicky was painfully charming, slightly effeminate, and a gormless weasel who had a malicious character. When Bernard had shore leave, the three of them would go out together. Bernard was naïve, believing that everyone was as honest as he was. He would thank Dicky for taking care of Jeanie while he was away and explain that he was grateful that she was being looked after by the Woods family. This delighted Dicky Woods no end. Bernard was a generous man and rewarded him handsomely for his dedication to Jeanie's wellbeing.

Over a period of three years, Jeanie had two children. Bernard Errington couldn't contain his joy when he arrived home to meet his tiny daughter Anna. He picked her up in his strong arms and admired the miracle that he had created. He was delighted that his little cherub looked like him, with big eyes and fair hair. However, it was different with Mary. She had none of Anna's delicate features. She was hard and angular. He had never known his grandparents, so he decided it was likely that Mary resembled one of them.

Dicky Woods broke the news that he was going to live with his old mum in Manchester.

"What? Why?" asked Jeanie.

"My ma needs someone to take care of her."

"I also need care," Jeanie whimpered before slumping her shoulders before him.

"Come now, love," said Dicky. "You know this had to come to an end."

"What are you saying? Will I never see you again?"

Dicky looked down at his shoes.

"Of course, you will. It's not far on the train."

Jeanie flew into his arms and buried her face in his chest.

"I need someone to look after me. I can't live alone."

Jeanie was beside herself.

"Look, love, you know that this can't continue forever. You have a husband."

"And the children?"

"Bernard will look after them. They will be fine."

Dicky held her, pacified her, and then showed her how much he would miss her.

Jeanie sank into a deep depression. Her best friend and lover had left. Jeanie didn't survive a month by herself. She stuffed her children's clothes into a bag without folding them, then went to the station and boarded a train for Manchester. The next time Bernard came home, he learned that his wife and children had moved to another city. Jeanie lost interest in everything. She had stopped caring years ago. Her husband was always at sea, her children were a nuisance, and she craved physical love.

She arrived on Dicky's doorstep, desperate. When Dicky saw her, he had mixed feelings. He desperately wanted to be free of her, but he couldn't find a woman even vaguely interested in him. At least Jeanie could manage to be a means to an end for the cad.

Bernard was disgusted when he saw the two rooms that his wife and children were living in. He made no bones about the fact that he was unhappy. That afternoon Dicky Woods popped in for tea. Bernard felt relieved.

"I agree, Bernard, it's not what she's used to, but at least I am here to look out for her."

When Bernard left, he shook Dicky's hand.

"Thank you, Dicky. I can rest knowing that you are here."

"Of course, Bernard. Anything for you."

Bernard took out some money, counted the notes and gave them to Dicky.

"I could never leave here without giving you something for your trouble."

"No, Bernard. That's not why I do it. You're my mate."

Bernard smiled at him.

"Have a pint or two on me next time you're in the pub."

*

Mavis McCrae pulled back the rag of a curtain and stared out of the dirty kitchen window. She was taking a good look at the bloke knocking on Jeanie Errington's door.

"'Ere, Elsie, that Dicky Wots-is-face is visiting Jeanie again."

"It's a disgrace if you ask me," answered her sister.

"I mean, who would want to look at Dicky Woods?

"Crikey O'Reilly, Mavis. The man has been in and out of there for about fifteen years. Does it still surprise you?"

"Ma Beckett says that Bernard knows, but he can't do anything about it," Mavis added, making her eyes wide and nodding her head.

"But Bernard is such a good man and smart as well. And I have heard that them blokes on the boats make good money," said a perplexed Elsie.

"Oh yes, Bernard Errington is a fine man. Yes, very smart in that uniform. And a good looker too."

"Do you know what's odd? Bernard often gets home when Dicky is visiting Jeanie. And you never hear a bad word come out of that man's mouth. There is never a rumpus between them two." Elsie said, shaking her head slowly. "Baffles me, it does."

"Well, I heard something interesting from Ma Beckett," said Mavis.

Elsie raised her eyebrows questioningly. Mavis yielded nothing. Her sister's curiosity made her impatient.

"Go on then, put me out of me misery!"

"Well, it goes something like this,"

Mavis stared out of the window and frowned like this was something that needed all her concentration.

"Nobody knows this," said Mavis.

"You know I am not a gossip," said Elsie

"Well, you know Ma Beckett reads cards and the tea leaves and all that. Well, she told me that Jeanie was in there some time ago, looking for one of those concoctions Ma Beckett makes."

"Oh my! What are you saying?"

"I think Jeanie is giving Bernard something to lose his wits."

Mavis nodded.

"And Ma Beckett told you this?"

"Well, not in so many words, but I put two and two together for myself."

"And Ma Beckett also does some magic, or so they say," said Elsie.

"Indeed. Elsie, we must be cautious around Jeanie. I would not drink a cuppa outa her kitchen if I was paid to. Ma Beckett is very good with those potions. You know how all that strange stuff works, so it does."

"I was thinking of telling Dicky. He works down at the Salvation Army, you know. Pity he is muddled up in this."

"What if Dicky is in on it?" asked Elsie

"I didn't think of it that way," Mavis mused aloud.

"And Dicky's old mother is moving. The old girl is also blind. She is going to live with her sister in Liverpool. Only the good Lord knows if she will make the trip," said Elsie

"Yea, Stella told me that she hasn't got long to go. Where will Dicky go? He has never left his mother's side, so he hasn't. He will be lost."

"Someone will surely take him in," said Elsie

"He does not get paid that much. But who can believe anything these days?"

"He probably gives all his money to Jeanie and her brats, Mavis."

"I have to get moving, Mavis. Me Tommy needs some dinner soon."

Elsie shuffled to the door. She lived six houses down from her sister, but it took her an hour to get home. By the time she arrived at her doorstep, the facts were clear: Dicky had been supporting Jeanie and her children for all these years, and Jeanie was feeding Bernard a concoction that was casting a spell over him.

*

When she returned from work one day, Mary looked at her mother in amazement.

"What did you say?"

"I said that I am taking Dicky Woods in as a boarder," said Jeanie in a sing-song voice.

"Why?"

"His mum, the dear old thing, is moving to Liverpool to be with her sister. She's blind, you know, and she can't get on with things like she used to, and—"

"Why?"

Mary cut her off mid-sentence.

"I need the money."

"No, you don't." Mary griped. "You get all of me Da's money, all of Anna's money, and I also pay my board and lodging. Those are mighty fine takings if you ask me."

"Well, I didn't ask you now, did I?" replied her curt mother.

"I've been doing some calculations, and all the money me Da earns could set us up in a decent house, and we could eat decent food."

"Cal-cu-la-tions." Jeanie enunciated the word. "You think you're so high and mighty using big words and fancy talk. I slaved to educate you, and this is how you repay me? I wish I had never put you in school."

"You have never slaved a day in your life, Ma. I went to the ragged school, and that was only after the welfare threatened you with gaol if you didn't send me."

"Always reminding me of my mistakes," Jeanie said sarcastically.

"So, where will you put him?"

"Who?" asked Jeanie, having lost the thread of the original conversation.

"Dicky Woods? Where will he sleep?"

"Here, in the kitchen. He's bringing his old cot with him. Bless his soul. It will be nice and warm in here."

"Yes, Ma, bless his soul indeed," spat Mary.

5

LOVE, POWER AND LIES

It was ten o'clock in the morning, and Colin Wheeler was already at the club having his fourth drink of the day. The sun was up, but the heavy cloud of soot and smoke that hovered over Salford turned the mighty star into a dull orange ball somewhere to the east.

The King George Club overlooked the large profitable dockyards of Manchester. The club was a seedy hole on the second floor of a building, condemned to be demolished. If you were invited to be a member, you could consider yourself one of the *'working-class elite'*. It was the hub of dockside political activity, and most nights, intense debates led to fisticuffs.

Shortly after the club opened, the members realised that exclusivity became rather dull. They began to ponder the benefit of the regular lower-class vices for entertainment. There was a vote, and the result was unanimous – the club would introduce gambling tables. Surpassing all expectations, it was agreed that women would be allowed entry at night too—but only if they were beautiful. By far, the greatest benefit of being a member was having a bar that was open twenty-four hours a day, including Sunday.

Colin reclined in a shabby velvet chair and studied the dock. The wharves were teeming with labourers, doing all manner of work. As Colin looked down upon this lot, he felt as if the world was at his feet, and he could be its master. The waiter, a young lad, called Jonesy had been replenishing Colin's whisky all morning, and Colin felt like King George himself.

Elated as he gazed across the Quays, Colin tried to calculate the amount of people working out there because he was angling towards forming a new labour union, and every penny would count. This union would provide more benefits for workers than the current one did, and his priority was to recruit and then gather a small union fee from every single man, woman and child who worked on the docks. He would easily inspire people to follow him. Colin would do it under the auspice of empowering, providing, and protecting the downtrodden working class. As the saying went, *'Rather get a little money from a million fools than a lot of money from one.'*

Of course, he would have some sort of low-level duty toward the members. That was easily managed. As with all unions, an annual strike accompanied by a small wage increase kept the labourers satisfied for a year. If the strike spiralled into violence and a few people got killed, it was an even greater success because it would put the government in a bad light. The more confrontation, the better. It was good for business. It reinforced the popular belief that the union would protect its members from the mighty empire in the name of justice, righteousness, and fairness. But, of course, it was all nonsense.

Colin knew that becoming a union leader was the only way that he would ever get rich. He had many friends who would manipulate any event if he asked them. It was easy to motivate the formulation of another workers union. All he had to do was exploit the working-class discontent. If he could influence the church to support him, marching under the banner of Christianity would be perfect. There would be a lot of money in the kitty, and as a dedicated, loyal leader, he needed proper remuneration for his troubles. Any righteous soul would agree that he was entitled to pay himself a reasonable salary, yet he couldn't appear too lavish, or it would raise eyebrows. Colin would have to practise self-control and live an understated lifestyle in England. He didn't want his wings clipping unnecessarily, though. The simple answer was to live humbly in Manchester and augment his earnings by funding the finest hotels in Paris, Berlin, Vienna, and New York from his generous expense account. He would go abroad for months at a time, under the auspices of fundraising, fighting the good fight for his boys. The plan suited him perfectly. Colin Wheeler would live a royal life.

His other priority was to find a hot-blooded, nubile young woman who would meet his physical needs while he stole from the poor to make himself rich. It didn't take long to find a hapless victim at St George's.

Colin caught a glimpse of Anna as she came into the club, stunned by her beauty and youth. Jonesy had told him that she was only seventeen. It irritated him that Anna was with the Portuguese greengrocer's son. He knew Mario Perreira from the docks, often seeing him delivering fresh produce for the ships. Many a time, Colin watched Mario operate. Almost every woman in the room fawned over the olive-skinned, brawny young man. In return, Mario made all the ladies that he met feel young, beautiful, and wanted. Unfortunately, Colin didn't possess that gift.

Mario couldn't keep his hands in his pockets, and he took every opportunity he had to touch Anna. It maddened Colin when he saw Mario run his swarthy hand down Anna's back. Colin had never been introduced to Anna, but it didn't stop him from jumping to his feet with the sole purpose of convincing Anna that he could offer her more than Perreira ever would.

Wheeler casually sauntered to the bar, tall, handsome, and confident. Colin was older than Mario and much more sophisticated. Comparing the two, Mario was a pretty boy and not a lot else.

The club was packed to capacity. The waiters weren't pouring drinks fast enough, and a queue formed at the bar counter. Punters were standing around the gambling tables, shouting out their bets, each person trying to outbid the other. There was a small group of musicians off to one side. The sound of the high-pitched harmonica and screeching fiddle grated on Colin's nerves. The over-exuberance of the crowd rubbed him up the wrong way, but he tolerated it because he planned to seduce Anna and humiliate Mario, and that was easier when he was in the same room.

Anna had perched herself on the arm of a faded chair, occupied by Shady Hawkins. Shady had earned her name by running the finest brothel in Salford, never revealing the identity of the wealthy clientele that she and her girls serviced. People who didn't know her so well called her Sandy.

> "Come and have tea at my office, darling," she cooed in Anna's ear.

The impressionable young girl couldn't believe that she had received an invitation from this sophisticated woman, who unbeknownst to her was also the most successful tart in Salford.

Colin reached Anna.

"Come now, Shady, the girl is with me."

He gave the woman a charming smile. Anna looked up into Colin's handsome face and frowned.

"Ah, hello Colin, how lovely to see you again!"

Shady glowed when she spoke to people, and Anna wanted to be just like her. Colin took Anna's hand and helped her to her feet.

"Excuse us, Shady," he said with a smile. "I have promised this young lady a meal."

Anna was perplexed.

"Have a lovely evening, Colin," Shady trilled, winking at him.

Colin ignored her and steered Anna through the drunken crowd until he had her on the landing.

"What are you doing?" Anna giggled.

"Rescuing you."

"Why?"

She laughed harder still, and her smile reached her twinkling eyes.

"The Portuguese boy is not your type, and neither is Shady."

"Mario and I are—"

Anna didn't finish the sentence.

"—Yes, I know."

Colin grabbed the girl's soft hand and pulled her down the stairs with him. Once on the dirty street, he whistled for a cab.

"Take us to the Dragon Arms," Colin instructed the driver.

"Are you hungry?" he asked.

"Starving," she giggled.

By midnight Anna was in Colin's bed. And by morning, Colin was hopelessly in love. Anna had exceeded all his expectations.

What Anna had not told either of her lovers, that she was two months pregnant with Mario's child. She didn't know what to do or where to seek advice, but eventually, she plucked up the courage to tell Mario that he was going to be a father.

Mario got to work later than usual. Anna was in a state of panic, forgetting that Mario did the late afternoon deliveries on a Wednesday. He climbed off the cart and walked into the warehouse, where they packed and cleaned the fruit and vegetables. Mario eyed Anna, busy scrubbing potatoes. He was furious with her. She had humiliated him when she flounced out of the club with Colin Wheeler, and European men didn't like being embarrassed by a woman.

Anna waited for the end of the day. Her nerves were shattered, and a few times, she considered not telling him at all, knowing that an illegitimate child would have a life of hell. It would be known as a 'desgraçado' for the rest of its life, ostracised for its mother's sins.

Anna cornered Mario after the last delivery. He knew something was wrong since she was not her usual vivacious self. He noted she looked drawn and exhausted. He glowered at her, then forced her to speak.

"What do you want with me?"

Anna shook her head and twisted her hands.

"What's wrong with you?" he barked at her.

"Mario, I am pregnant."

He went quiet, and he began unloading the wagon.

"I won't marry you. You are not the wife I want."

Anna burst into tears.

"You know how it works in the family. You know I would never marry the likes of a woman like you. You are not even a Catholic."

Eventually, Mario looked her straight in the eye. The warm, charming young man she once knew was gone, replaced by a ruthless monster.

> "I don't want you, and I don't want the desgraçado. Get out of here, and never come back."

She ran as far away from Mario as she could manage. Back at home, Anna was beside herself. She struggled to eat the broth that her mother had prepared. Jeanie served the meal with fresh, crispy bread and smooth, creamy butter. What was usually cooked as a treat made Anna want to wretch. So many of her friends had warned her against Mario. Even Mary had told her that she was stupid. She had not listened to anyone.

Now, she had met Colin Wheeler, who adored her. She liked him but couldn't muster any stronger feelings for him. How would she tell him that she was pregnant with another man's child? He would not want her anymore. She had destroyed her life. Now, she had no work, the baby would be illegitimate, and the one chance she had to marry well was ruined.

*

Mario's mother bent over the big dining room table and shook her finger at him.

> "I told you to leave that girl alone. She is no good. She is not Portuguese. She is not a Catholic."

Mario and his father were both silent while Mama Perreira raged on.

"That is not your child, do you hear me, Mario? That is not your child. If that girl sleeps with you, well, she gets into any man's bed. It is not your child."

"But Mama, it is mine," Mario said quietly.

"Then you pay Ma Beckett to get rid of it," she cried.

"But Mama!" Mario protested. "We can't do that. It's against our religion."

"She is not a Catholic. It does not matter."

Mario's father put his hand on Mario's arm and signalled him to be quiet.

"Stop being so angry, Mama," said Mr Perreira in a placating tone.

"We can keep the child. Raise it in our family. You know how important family is to us, Mama."

This comment evoked more rage from Mario's mother.

"Nao! Nao! It will bring shame upon us. Mario must marry a virgin, or the church will never consecrate the marriage, and he will die in hell."

Mr Perreira didn't say a word.

"Take the *'prostituta'* to Ma Beckett. She will get rid of the *'desgraçado'*."

Mario and his father were terrified of Mama's wrath, especially when she gave the cruel instruction to end its life:

"Arrancar do útero!"

Mario walked to Angel Street. On the one hand, he hated his mother for dominating him. On the other, she was making his life easy. Mario had enjoyed Anna sexually, and he knew that they had no future when he took her to bed. He only wanted her as another conquest for his libido. He would pay for the abortion, hoping the scandal would escape the wagging tongues of the Portuguese community. If anyone dared get wind of this story, he would struggle to find a wife from a good family.

Mario knocked on the door, and Jeanie opened it.

"Aww, me darling, how are you?" she drawled.

Mario was revolted by her, but he gave her a dazzling smile to get what he wanted.

"I need to speak to Anna."

Anna heard Mario's voice from the bedroom. She came into the front room and smiled, half hoping that he had come to his senses and she would at least have her job back. Anna put on her coat.

"Where are you going, lass? It's icy out there."

Anna ignored her mother, who wanted her to mind her own business and not someone else's as usual. The frosty couple walked to the end of the rows before he spoke.

"I will meet you and Ma Beckett, Tuesday afternoon. She will remove it."

Anna looked at him aghast.

"It?"

"I will pay. Nobody will know."

"Is this what you want?" Anna interrogated.

"Yes. And it is what Mama and Papa want too. The matter is settled."

Mario met Anna down the side street by Ma Beckett's house. It was a miserable day, a reflection of how Anna was feeling. The poor girl was terrified. The two of them walked down a dirty lane between two housing rows. She reached the back-to-back and knocked. The old woman opened the door, and Anna stepped in.

"You will sleep here tonight," were the first words Ma Beckett spoke.

"Why?"

"I will have to be near when you start to bleed. Can't have you dying. Causes all sorts of bother."

"Oh," whispered Anna.

"Take off your draws and get on the table. I want to see how far you are."

There were no niceties or kindness. The old woman behaved as though she had never seen the girl before, although they had bumped into each other many times running errands. Anna studied the woman. Ma Beckett was hunched and wrinkled. She had a long, thin, crooked nose. Her long, straight grey hair was knotted under a bonnet. She had lost a few teeth, and her long fingernails had dirt under them. Anna got onto the table, the same table where Ma Beckett ate. She watched the woman go over to a bucket and pull out a thin iron rod.

"Open your legs and pull them up," Ma Beckett instructed mechanically like a surgeon in a public operating theatre.

Anna felt beside herself with shame. She had never had anyone look at her except Mario and didn't know what to expect. She was terrified and humiliated. The woman pushed and prodded Anna's stomach.

"The baby is far along. At least two months."

Anna nodded.

"Is it quickening?"

Anna looked baffled by the term.

"Answer the question, girl. Does it move?"

Anna nodded.

"Then it will cost more."

Anna didn't know what to say. This didn't bother Ma Beckett. She knew that the Perreira family had a lot of money, and they would pay anything to get their beloved son out of trouble.

Anna pulled down her dress and sat up.

"I am not finished. Lie back down," the old crone said, shoving her.

Anna lay down again. Ma Beckett stood between Anna's legs. Without warning, the woman took her dirty fingers and put them into the birth canal. Anna screamed.

"Shut up. Do you want the Peelers to hear you?"

Anna's eyes began to water, and tears ran down her face and dripped onto the table.

"Stop your sniffling. You should have thought about this when you let that boy near you. It's too late to cry about it now, stupid girl."

Ma Beckett pushed and poked until she was satisfied. She had felt everything that she could.

"The child is bigger than I thought. Why didn't you come earlier?"

"I was afraid."

Ma Baker cackled:

"Ha, they all say that."

Then she shook her head in disgust. Anna began to cry again. The judgement was harsh.

"I will give you something to drink. Go lie on the floor over there." She pointed to a dingy corner of the room, the flagstones plastered with all sorts of filth.

"When you start to bleed, I will do the rest."

"The rest?" Anna asked in hardly a whisper.

"Yes, I will likely have to use the instruments to get it out."

Ma Beckett brewed up one of her special teas, poured it into a cracked beaker, then handed it to Anna.

"Drink it all, every last drop. Do you hear me?" the woman said, no kindness in her voice."

"Are you going to use that thing on me?"

Anna pointed at the rod.

"I'll have to, yes."

"What will you do with it?"

"You really are a stupid little wench. Why I'll put it in the same place where Mario Perreira put his—"

Anna didn't wait for the woman to finish the sentence. She got off the table with as much dignity as she could and put on her draws. She pulled her dress down and looked at the filthy old woman in front of her. She felt hatred for Ma Beckett, and she never wanted to see the evil witch again.

"Where are you going?" said Ma Beckett in an eerie voice.

"You're not sticking your filthy hands in me again. Never again."

"What about the money? You can't get going without paying me."

"I owe you nothing."

She stood in front of the door and would not let Anna leave.

"Get out of my way!" screamed Anna.

Ma Beckett gave her a sly smile. Anna felt angry and humiliated. She had been violated by this woman, and there was nothing she could do about it.

"I want me money," said Ma Beckett menacingly, guarding the door.

Anna lifted her hand and slapped Ma Beckett. Her flat hand landed on the old woman's ear, and temporarily she felt off-balance. She gave way in front of the door. Anna opened the door and ran through Angel Meadows like a wild animal and would not stop until it felt safe.

Mario saw her running and chased after her. Eventually, he caught up with the girl and grabbed her arm, spinning her around to face him.

"What do you think you are doing."

"I don't care what your family says," Anna said, panting, "I will never do what you want."

"You will. I will force you."

Anna had felt empowered after slapping Ma Beckett. She lifted her arm and slapped Mario twice, putting all her weight behind it, then she ran home. There was nowhere else to go. She contemplated telling Mary, but her sister would likely have the same attitude as Mrs Perreira. She couldn't tell her mother. Jeanie would tell Dicky, who would tell everybody he knew.

Colin had not seen Anna for two weeks, and he was beside himself with concern. He had gone to Perreira Grocer's to look for her, but he was told Anna didn't work there anymore. He had never visited Anna at home, but he knew where she lived on Angel Street. It was midwinter and blowing a blizzard. The snow piled against the blackened buildings. Temporarily, the Meadows were bright. Colin put his hand up to shield his face from the stinging cold and fought his way to Anna's house.

"Dear God!" exclaimed Jeanie when she saw the stranger. "Who are you?"

Colin pushed through the door as he gave his name, grateful for the warmth of the fire in the small room.

"Do you want to kill yourself in this weather?"

"No, no," muttered Colin. "May I please speak to Anna?"

"Anna," shouted Jeanie. "You have a visitor."

Jeanie studied Colin from top-to-toe. He spoke far more eloquently than she did. He was well dressed and seemed to have good manners. If this was the type of man Mary brought home, Jeanie would be doubly delighted.

Anna's eyes widened when she saw Wheeler, thrown into an instant state of anxiety. She didn't know what to say to him.

"How about some tea?" asked Jeanie.

Colin smiled at Anna's mother.

"A cup of tea will be lovely. But can you give me a moment with Anna first, then we can all sit down and get warm?"

Jeanie was spellbound. She had not met many men like this. In fact, the last one who had a shred of good breeding about him was her husband, Bertie.

"Of course, of course."

Jeanie went into the other room and pulled the curtain across the doorway, then Colin rushed toward Anna and pulled her into his arms.

"Where have you been, child? Are you sick? Why did you leave your job?"

Anna was overwhelmed by all the questions. She didn't want to face him.

"I am pregnant. Three? Four months? I don't know. A while," Anna blurted out before bursting into tears.

The day had been too much for her. She felt fragile and lonely. Colin stepped back and looked at her. He lifted both his arms and pushed his hands through his hair. Anna could see his mind calculating the months. She saw the shock on his face when he realised that he was not the father.

"Is Mario the father?"

"Yes."

"I went to Ma Beckett's this afternoon."

"Who is that?"

"She's an old woman here in The Meadows who, who—" Anna was at a loss for an explanation. "She gets rid of babies."

"But that could have killed you," Colin gasped.

"I know. It was terrible. I ran away just before she was going to start."

Colin held her closely, loving being a hero and a saviour.

"Oh, Anna, never do anything that stupid again. Do you hear me? I love you, Anna. You may feel all alone, but I love you."

Anna didn't believe that she heard these words. It was the most ridiculous display of emotion.

"Do you love me?" asked Colin

"I do," Anna lied.

"Well, I love you more than anything in the world. I will marry you and the baby."

He laughed. The idea was staggering, but to him, it made perfect sense. Anna looked stunned as Colin swept her up in his arms.

"What's happening?" shouted Jeanie and went into the front room.

Just then, the front door creaked open, and a half-frozen Mary stumbled into the room. She barely had time to take in the scene. A respectable-looking man was standing in the front room of her mother's house, with his arms around Anna and their mother staring at them with a great big smile.

"I have asked Anna to marry me," Colin shouted joyfully.

Mary looked from her sister to her mother with bewilderment.

"What did she say? What did she say?" asked Jeanie, jumping up and down like a skipping child.

Colin looked at Anna in absolute adoration, then he smiled broadly.

"She said yes!"

6

THE ANNOUNCEMENT

The news of Anna's wedding rapidly reached the ears of Jeanie's neighbours.

"Bleedin' hell," Mavis cursed.

"Well, I'll be a monkey's uncle," said Elsie, clapping her hand over her mouth.

"Do you think we will be invited to the wedding?"

"I am sure we will, but I think it will be a very small affair," said Elsie trying to sound posh. "They'll go down to the registry office then a few toots at the local."

"Yes, and probably at The Dragon," Mavis agreed.

"Yes," nodded Elsie as she stroked her chin. "That would be wise."

"And then I suppose back to work for them."

"Just wondering about something," said Elsie slyly. "Do you think Anna is in the family way?"

"We'll see when the baby gets here," Mavis chuckled. "The dates don't lie."

The Salford Daily reported that one hundred and fifty guests attended the wedding of Mr and Mrs Colin Wheeler. They were married in the fine cathedral on Victoria Street, and the reception was held at the less fine St George's Club. Afterwards, the lucky couple were travelling to London for their honeymoon.

The guest list was a reflection of and tribute to Colin's growing popularity and resources. He had invited all the people whom he wished to impress. His friends assured him that the wedding would be featured in the social columns of the Sunday newspapers, just like the nobility would. This would serve to introduce him to the upper crust.

"There is a new word in politics, Colin. It's called publicity. The days of standing on a soapbox in the market square are over. Now we build our image in the press," said Raleigh Peterson, a journalist from the Daily Herald.

Anna looked beautiful. She glowed like an angel in the beautiful dress that she wore. She was oblivious of her role as a political tool for the day. Colin realised that his wife needed some refinement if they were to advance socially, but a few lessons in etiquette would easily solve that problem. Colin didn't come from a wealthy family, but the Wheeler's were well known and respected in Manchester.

Mary studied her sister, thinking how easy it was for some people to get ahead when the cards fell in their favour. Anna didn't need intelligence or skill: she had a beautiful face and body. Mary didn't miss anything. She also noticed that Anna was more curvaceous than usual. As Anna was introduced to the guests, her warmth and sincerity captured their hearts. Mary, on the other hand, had none of that easy charm, and she knew it.

She glanced at her mother. Jeanie looked very presentable in a new dress and pretty hat. Both items were tasteful. Dicky Woods stood next to her, decked out in a new suit. His waistcoat was bright and cheerful, and his white-collar was starched to perfection. Mary noted that Dicky was very interested in the time. He kept on removing a rather expensive-looking fob watch from its pocket and glancing at it. Mary realised that watch was new, and he was trying to show it off. Her blood boiled. The watch could only have been paid for by one person. Her mother.

Mary wished that Bernard Errington had been in attendance to give Anna away. He would have cut a fine figure in his spotless uniform and peaked cap under his arm. Mary's mind drifted onto the subject of her own nuptials.

Mary was adamant that her marriage would have a purpose, believing that wealth and social influence were the only motivation for entering into the arrangement. Mary had no intention of handing her hard-earned fortune to any man, so he had better arrive with his own. Children? What was society's fixation with breeding? Mary would have to agree to have children. She would be forced to give birth again and again until she produced a son. Men were obsessed with leaving a legacy. All Mary wanted to do was work hard, get rich and then fall into eternal blissful sleep. If she ever married, she hoped that she and her husband would be like-minded people. For her, the ideal man she wanted to marry would be happy to settle for one child. If she was lucky—none.

Mary left the party unnoticed. There were better things to do. Time was money. Every time Alec Riddle shoved money into her fist, it was one step closer to freedom. Soon, she would be free from the putrid streets of Angel Meadows. Nobody understood the stench of poverty. It permeated the air around you. It stuck to your clothing. If you allowed it, it would rot you from the inside out. That was a fate she went to great lengths to avoid.

Alec Riddle smiled as he let Mary into his small apartment.

"Hello. What are you doing here so early? I thought you would be at the wedding?"

"I couldn't tolerate all of that wretched happiness," answered Mary wryly.

Alec laughed. Over the years, he had become accustomed to Mary's dry humour.

All that Alec Riddle ever wanted from Mary was an untarnished lover who would not give him the clap. His wife had died a few years earlier, and he had physical needs. His expectation was that there be a mutual respect between him and Mary, but the relationship developed beyond his expectations and Alec fell deeply in love. Alec wanted to propose marriage. As lovers, they were compatible and satisfied with each other. Mary was the most brilliant young woman that he had ever met. If she accepted the proposal, Alec knew that it would never be a conventional marriage. Mary would never be a wife in the true sense of the word. She would never scrub and clean or pop out endless numbers of children, nor would she indulge his every whim.

Alec knew he had to hatch a brilliant plan to coax her into marriage, and he was relieved when he stumbled across the solution. He would send Mary to university. She would read the law. Mary would graduate as a solicitor or a barrister, and they would build an empire.

Mary's relationship with Alec was a monument to her pragmatism. She appreciated that Alec Riddle was older, but he was handsome and virile. He treated her with respect and kindness. They both focused on satisfying each other's desires, and she enjoyed it. Above all, he was intellectually challenging, and she loved a challenge.

Mary lay in Alec's arms, satisfied. This was the only time that she allowed herself the luxury of human comfort. Her thick hair flowed over her shoulders. She looked soft and feminine, a characteristic she disguised by her harsh mannerisms and dress.

"I want to marry you," said Alec directly.

Alec felt Mary's body stiffen.

"I don't love you."

Alec knew that all along, of course, but he was surprised how much the words stung. He didn't believe that Mary could or would ever feel the heady emotion of love. She had been born with every gift and sense, except the one to feel emotion.

"You don't have to love me, Mary. In return for you giving me your company, I have an offer for you to consider."

Alec knew that he would have to present a good case to win her over. He had to make her an offer, something she couldn't resist.

"I want to build a powerful law firm, and I want you beside me. We will go and live out in Cheshire, and I will send you to university to become a lawyer."

Mary lifted her head and looked at him. Alec had her attention.

"I expect nothing extra of you. We will have a relationship as we do now. I don't want children. My first and only child died, I never want to suffer that loss again. I have mourned in this dreary hole for long enough. I am ready to begin again. You can have your own bedroom. You can come to me when you choose, but I want you to be my wife."

"Why?" asked Mary.

Alec's answer would be vital to her decision, and he knew it.

"I trust you," he said.

Alec was sincere. He did trust Mary. She had kept their secret for years. She could easily have blackmailed him, given him over to the authorities or gossiped. The word 'trust' resonated with Mary. She began her own unique proposal.

"I shall be allowed to amass my own fortune?"

"Yes."

He smiled as he stroked her face. Mary didn't realise his tenderness as she negotiated the details of her prenuptial agreement.

"I can retain my own estate. It won't become your property?"

"Yes."

"And you will sign a contract to that effect?"

"Yes, I will."

"As you know, I don't want to be poor—I want to be rich."

Propping his head on his hand, Alec turned to smile at her. Mary lay and stared at the ceiling, weighing up the pros and cons of the offer.

"I will pay you back for the university tuition," she said.

"No," he said, gazing down at her. "It's a wedding gift."

Mary gave a rare smile, and Alec's heart soared.

"Alright then. Yes," said Mary. "I can agree to matrimony as long we are in agreement on the terms and conditions."

Alec laughed loudly. His fiancée certainly knew how to negotiate. He kissed her passionately, and she responded in the same way. Mary couldn't share emotions, but she could share her body.

Mary walked home. She saw nothing around her. For once, the untoward scenes of whores, pimps, drunks, dead and dying were invisible. She could ignore the smell of the tannery, the blood-soaked shambles, diseased pig styes and open sewers. Mary's entire being had transcended Angel Meadows. She saw the future clearly. She would build an empire. She couldn't love Alec, but he was her best friend. She would be his partner for as long as she could trust him. She was experiencing hope. She just didn't recognise it.

Mary had no desire to tell her mother about the proposal. She could imagine Jeanie's gushing 'ohs' and 'ahs', and she would not be able to stomach it. Moreover, she would most certainly never introduce Alec to her family.

Mary reached the door of the back-to-back where she had lived since she was a small child. A soft yellow glow emanated from under the door, giving the false impression of warmth and comfort inside.

Dicky and Jeanie were well past jolly when Mary left the party. She was convinced that Jeanie would be passed out by now. Dicky Woods could still be awake. The doorpost was swollen from the rain. Mary gave the door a bump with her hip to force it open. The front room was empty, but a welcoming oil lamp was standing on the old kitchen table, glowing a rich amber. Dicky's cot was empty. She was hardly one step into the room when she heard groans from the room that she and her mother shared.

Mary pushed aside the dirty, ragged curtain that separated the room. Stood in the doorway, the light was dim, and she had difficulty making sense of what she was seeing. Her eyes became accustomed to the light. Jeanie was lying on Mary's cot, and Dicky Woods was thrusting himself into her, her legs wrapped around his back. They were groaning with pleasure. Something in Jeanie's subconscious must have alerted her that there was someone else in the room. Mid-groan, she opened her eyes wide and stopped moving. It was instinctual, like an animal aware of the danger. Dicky kept on thrusting.

It took Jeanie a moment to recognise the shadow in the doorway as Mary. Jeanie tried to shove Dicky off her, but he couldn't stop himself.

"Mary, Mary!" Jeanie cried from underneath Dicky.

The scene was surreal. Mary began to back out of the room, but her eyes were riveted on them.

"Come back, Mary. Don't leave," shouted Jeanie over Dicky's shoulder.

Given the circumstances, the mother's request was obscene. She met her mother's eyes.

"What else can I do?" cried Jeanie. "I am lonely."

It was the filthiest image that Mary would ever witness. The streets of Angel Meadows were a constant challenge to morality, but this was incomparable to anything she had been exposed to. Mary knew that she would have to work very hard to erase this experience, or it would haunt her for the rest of her life, constantly reminding her of where she came from.

Mary watched her mother, naked and terrified, trying to justify herself to her daughter as she lay impaled under Dicky Woods.

The girl showed no emotion. She fetched the kitchen knife. She wanted the satisfaction of plunging the knife into the exposed back of Dicky Woods, again and again, until his body went limp. A glint of light off the sharp blade brought her to her senses. As always, logic prevailed, and she stopped herself. She would not ruin her life for the sake of Jeanie. Her father's hard-earned money was going into supporting her mother and the filthy dog she lay with. Mary felt a fiery hatred consume her and settle in the middle of her chest hotter than a burning brazier by the dockside. She would have left immediately, but something deterred her. Her savings were hidden in the wall behind the cot.

When Dicky's body finally collapsed on top of Jeanie, he realised her cries weren't of pleasure but distress. He looked over his shoulder and saw Mary. He grabbed the blanket and pulled it over his white, pasty body. Jeanie was all arms and legs as she pushed him off her.

"How long has she been stood there?" Dicky screamed at Jeanie.

"I don't know. I opened my eyes, and she was there."

Jeanie collapsed into sobs.

"Get out of here," Dicky screamed at Mary. "Do not stand there gawking. I'll break yer bloody neck, so I will. Get the hell away."

Then, Dicky saw the knife and realised that he was lucky to be alive. Mary turned and walked a few feet into the front room. She put the knife on the table.

"She will tell her father," cried Jeanie, "then what will we do?"

"Shut yer gob, Jeanie. Shut it."

Mary listened to them shouting at each other.

"If she finds out about the debt, she will tell Bernard. Then where will we be?" Jeanie sobbed uncontrollably.

"Get dressed and act normal, you bleedin' id-iot."

It was a strange place to experience a rare flash of humour, but Dicky telling her mother to act normal was curiously amusing.

Jeanie came rushing out of the room stinking of alcohol and other body odours. She ran toward Mary, arms outstretched, wanting to comfort her daughter.

"Get away from me."

"I am sorry," said Jeanie. "It's the first time, I promise Mary, it is the first time."

"What have you spent my father's money on?"

Mary had no interest in her mother's promiscuity, only the money. Dicky glared at Jeanie, willing her to shut up.

"Dicky has needed help starting a small business. He is brilliant, you know?"

Mary stared her down.

"He needed a little help. It is really a good investment, could make us thousands."

Mary's silence was intimidating Jeanie, and she blundered on.

"Yes, we ran up some gambling debts together."

"And he needed a suit for the wedding," said Mary sarcastically. "And a new watch."

"We couldn't leave him on the street. He would have died of cold and hunger. Your father wouldn't allow it. His old mother left him behind. He had nothing."

"And my da agreed with this?" asked Mary.

Jeanie stared at the floor.

"You are the laughing stock of the rows, Ma."

Jeanie put her head in her hands and started to sob again.

"Stop your crying," said Mary coldly. "You have nothing to cry about."

"Do not talk to yer Ma like that, you harpy," shouted Dicky.

"Get your stuff together and get out of my father's house," said Mary calmly.

"Your father? Your father?" asked Dicky in a soft, menacing voice.

"Are you sure he is your father?"

"Stop, Dicky, Stop!" Jeanie cried out.

Mary looked from Dicky to her mother. Dicky had a sardonic smile on his face.

"Tell me," said Mary, unemotional, just wanting the facts.

"No," cried Jeanie hysterically.

"Tell me," roared Mary.

Dicky laughed loudly.

Jeanie's sobs became louder.

"Shut up, Jeanie. You're getting on my nerves." Dicky ordered.

He turned and pushed himself against Mary. She could smell his putrid breath against her cheek.

"You're a big lass now, Mary. You understand these things."

Dicky laughed and winked at her. Mary looked at the knife on the table. She was wrestling with the decision to murder him while her mother sat a crumpled heap on the kitchen chair. She pushed him away from her. Dicky was surprised by her strength.

"Is it true?"

Mary couldn't find it in herself to call the woman 'mother'.

"Who is my father?"

Jeanie's eyes moved to Dicky.

"Him?" asked Mary in wonderment.

Dicky put his head back and laughed loudly.

"Don't you dare, Dicky," screeched Jeanie. We will never get another cent from Bernard.

"She had better behave herself then," warned Dicky.

"You have lied to us for all these years?"

She looked at her mother with the same steely gaze as a hawk. Jeanie would not raise her head and stared at the floor and cried in shame. She just managed a few pathetic nods. Mary couldn't believe what she was hearing. Bernard Errington had provided for them all these years, and she wasn't his child. She had been cheated out of the father she respected, and Bernard Errington had been cheated out of his money for all these years. Mary felt her father was an idiot for being so trusting. She couldn't quantify the situation emotionally but could logically. Bernard Errington might not be her real father, but he deserved to be reimbursed.

She had heard enough. She went into her annexe room and drew the curtain behind her. Taking out her tatty carpetbag, she put a few things in it. She pushed the cot to one side and removed the skirting board, then put her hand in the hole. She bent her arm awkwardly until she felt the tin in her hand. Reassuringly heavy, it comforted her. She placed it in the bag between her clothes. She saw Dicky's expensive watch that Bernard Errington had unwittingly paid for. She picked up both and went into the front room. Dicky was too raving mad to notice what Mary was up to.

"Where are you going," demanded Jeanie.

Mary didn't reply.

"How will I survive?" called her pathetic mother, thinking about herself and her foibles as usual.

Mary walked to the stove, opened the door, and stuffed the suit into it. She watched until it began to smoulder.

"What are you doing?" Dicky screamed at her. "That cost a bloody fortune."

He stepped toward her, his first curled. Mary didn't flinch. Something about her cold eyes made him stop. Then the girl threw something onto the floor. It glimmered in the low light. Dicky realised it was the watch. He dived onto all fours trying to rescue it but couldn't reach it in time. The watch was inches away from Dicky. Mary brought her boot down upon it, and the glass shattered. She stamped on it repeatedly until the cogs and springs pinged their way out of the casing. All that remained was the distorted silver that used to be the case. Dick knew that he could still get something for the precious metal and reached out his hand to take it. Mary brought her foot down on his fingers, and he screamed in agony. She bent down and picked up what was left of the casing. She picked up the carpetbag, opened the door, and stepped into the stinking alley.

"Come back this moment," she heard Jeanie scream behind her.

Dicky followed her out of the house. Mary deliberately walked past the privies, with Dicky close on her heel. She took the piece of silver in her hand and tossed it into the courtyard. It landed in the mud, slime, and faeces that hid the cobbles. Dicky ran past her, dropped onto his hands and knees, and shoved his fingers into the stinking debris, hunting around in desperation.

Mary turned and left. She saw the Scuttlers leaning against the walls, wearing flat caps, scarves and brass tipped clogs. She removed a substantial amount of money from her pocket and whispered a few words to one of them.

She watched them approach Dicky from behind. He was distracted, oblivious to anything around him. It was quick and easy. They kicked him twice, then beat his head in with a lead pipe. Mary felt nothing as she watched Dicky Woods die. She had not murdered him. He had died of greed.

She had no father. The man had never existed. She had liberated herself. Her thoughts were already on the future. She would not look back. She would never look back.

Mary walked from Angel Meadows to Churchill Road. When she got to Alec Riddle's address, she unlocked the street door with the key that he had given her many years ago. She climbed the stairs to his apartment and knocked loudly. She heard fumbling inside, then a dishevelled Alec opened the door. When he saw Mary, he smiled.

"I am on my way to work," said Mary.

"This early?"

"Yes, I am going to ask Mr Porter for the day off."

Alec frowned.

"Are you ill?" he asked, concerned.

"No, Alec."

She managed a smile:

"We are getting married this afternoon."

Mary and sat behind Alec's desk. She took a sheet of paper from his top drawer and picked up a pen. She dipped it into the navy blue ink and began to write.

To Anna,

It has come to my attention that Dicky Woods is our father, not Bernard Errington.

I hope that this information will be of use in the future.

I have taken care of the situation.

Yours sincerely,

Mary had no regrets after she penned the letter. Her sister was too big for her boots, and the lie would bring her down to earth. The beautiful Anna needed to be taken down a notch or two.

The neighbours found Dicky the next morning. They weren't surprised that someone had finished him off. A well-known rogue, he owed everybody money. His body was put on a cart and taken up the hill to St Michael's. Jeanie collapsed in the street when she saw his corpse, the love of her life was dead. Who would look after her now? Mavis and Elsie took her home and tried to comfort her, but it was of no use. The funeral was small, Dicky was not a popular man, and the minister had very little to say about him except that 'he was a good man and would be missed'. Neither statement was true.

Jeanie's daughters no longer visited her. Mary never wanted to see her again, and Anna had a new life with her husband. Jeanie took to her bed, eating less and less. Mavis and Elsie tried to force-feed her but with no success. Jeanie became weaker and weaker until she couldn't stand up. On a bitterly cold night, with temperatures below zero, she had no energy to put coal into the stove and warm the rooms. When Mavis went to check on her a few days later, they found her dead, frozen to death.

7

ILLEGITIMATE

Anna opened the letter. All the blood drained from her face, and she felt light-headed. It couldn't be true. She hated Dicky Woods, and now she was told that he was her father. She felt ashamed down to her soul, filthy and alien to herself. She was no longer Anna Errington. She was Anna Woods. Her head was spinning, and her thoughts raging. How would this information help her in the future? Her sister was full of malice. How had she taken care of the situation? Anna couldn't look at herself in the mirror without seeing Dicky Woods. She turned to the only person who loved her and whom she trusted, her husband.

Colin read the note and collapsed into a chair. He put his head back and stared at the ceiling. He loved Anna, but she had brought a lot of problems with her. He began to wonder if he had been wise to marry her. He turned her head and looked into her eyes, which were brimming with tears.

> "You know that I love you and that this means nothing to me," he reassured.

Anna nodded, unable to speak.

> "I will handle this right now, my darling. I will burn this letter immediately and never think of it again."

Anna tried to smile as tears streamed down her contorted face. Colin went next door to his office with the note. But he didn't burn it. He put it in his desk drawer, then took a poker and prodded the coals in grate noisily.

Anna's belly was growing by the day. Colin paraded her about, satisfied to accept congratulations and wallow in the attention to his virility. The marriage to Colin had lifted Anna one rung up the social ladder. Everyone thought that she was lovely, but Anna was uncomfortable. She couldn't forget her humble roots and struggled to be pretentious. She was completely overwhelmed to be in the public eye.

Colin launched the new trade union shortly after their wedding. Anna watched him giving speeches at the dockside, pubs, and clubs. Colin would address workers outside the tanneries, cotton mills, match factories, and Anna watched him with admiration but not love. In contrast, Colin couldn't get enough of his beautiful wife.

"Anna, my angel, the people adore you," Colin said, putting his arms around her.

Anna would laugh softly, her eyes bright and her face glowing.

"You are going to make me very famous," laughed Colin and took another sip of the cheap Scotch that he was drinking.

"Thank you," Anna whispered.

The following morning, over breakfast, Anna opened the newspaper. She saw a small article. There had been a murder in Angel Meadows. A man, Dicky Woods, had been beaten to death. Anna had a horrible feeling she knew what Mary meant when she said she had taken care of him, and prayed she was wrong.

Mr and Mrs Wheeler were living in a three-bedroomed house on the better side of Salford. It was not a mansion, but it was a palace if you were raised in The Meadows. Colin bought Anna new clothes, gave her access to a cab, and had her visit a respectable doctor. Three women worked in the house. They knew Anna's humble background. Anna could also identify with them, and because she didn't behave like an upstart, they helped her as much as they could. They were more like a small band of friends than servants.

Anna felt lost. She had no family. Her mother was dead. It had come as a shock, and Anna couldn't contain her sorrow. She had stood and watched her mother's coffin lowered into the water-filled grave, and Colin steadied her, afraid that she would collapse. Anna tried to find Mary, but her sister had vanished. Out of desperation, she went to see Mr Porter.

"I am sorry about your mother, Mrs Wheeler." Mr Proctor said kindly.

He studied Anna carefully. He recognised a warm heart and kindness in her that Mary didn't have. It always surprised him how different siblings could be, even his own children.

"Mr Porter, I am looking for Mary."

There was concern in Anna's voice.

"Mary gave her notice a few months ago."

"Did she say where she was going? Did she find another position?"

"She said she was getting married."

"Oh, my word," stammered Anna. "Who was she going to marry?"

"I only know that he is a solicitor, and his name is Riddle. They have moved to Manchester where Mr Riddle will practise law, while your sister attends the Faculty of Law at Manchester University."

Mary had asked Mr Porter to keep the information confidential, but he felt sorry for Anna. She seemed lonely and vulnerable, especially after the recent loss of her mother.

Anna couldn't believe what she was hearing. All this time, Mary had kept this secret to herself, but it was typical of her sister.

"If you hear anything about her whereabouts, will you please let me know?"

"Of course, Mrs Wheeler," Mr Porter said formally.

"Please call me Anna. Everyone else does."

Mr Porter smiled at the beautiful, humble girl, who was married to one of the most powerful men in Manchester.

"Of course, lass, I will let you know."

Everything was happening as Colin had planned, but there was a problem, Anna was around seven months pregnant, and they were only married for three. Thankfully Anna was carrying small, which was a blessing. She managed to hide the bulge well under layers and layers of winter clothes, but it was becoming more difficult.

"It's time for you to go to Ireland, Anna. Remember we discussed this before?" said Colin, stroking her hair.

Anna nodded.

"You will need to be away for a good amount of time, Anna. Nobody must get wind of the situation."

Anna had agreed to this plan from the beginning.

"What about Mario Perreira?" asked Anna.

"He will never say a word, sweetheart."

"If he tells anyone, our lives will be ruined."

Colin knew that Anna was correct.

"Mario had become engaged to a young Portuguese woman. The Perreiras won't allow this to become popular news."

"And if they do?"

"I will take care of the Perreira family. You never have to fear them," said Colin, holding Anna protectively.

Although Anna didn't love him, she enjoyed the security he brought.

"What will you do if he threatens to squeal?" asked Anna

"If I get wind of any ill intentions, I will burn his business to the ground. That will stop him from having a loose tongue. It will ruin his family."

Anna gasped, shocked by Colin's ruthlessness.

"Nobody will hurt you, Anna. I promise," he reinforced, although it didn't ease her worries.

Colin and Anna agreed that she would leave for Dublin as soon as possible. She would travel under the auspices of going to visit a needy friend. Dublin was in chaos, and it was unlikely that she would meet anyone whom they knew. Once there, she would live in a boarding house under a false name and say that her husband had died.

"Don't make them feel too sorry for you, Anna. You don't want to draw too much attention to yourself," Colin quipped.

Anna was anxious to play the role of a widow, and the idea of travelling to Dublin by herself was terrifying. She had never been beyond Salford.

"You must stay there for three months after the baby is born. We will register the birth in England when you get back. That way, we can diddle the dates a little."

The night Anna departed for Dublin, Colin held her as though he would never see her again. He swore his love to her and made endless promises that he wouldn't remember.

The Liverpool wharf teemed with people waiting to board the Dublin ferry. Anna was dressed plainly, just a young pregnant woman going off to take care of her ill relative. The weather out of Liverpool was fair, and the sea was smooth. Anna's maiden voyage, she had never set foot on a ship before. The young woman stared at everything in wonderment. She was beautiful, and she couldn't stop smiling. Everyone commented on the glowing young pregnant woman as she walked on deck.

The ferry moved out of the harbour. They drifted away from the land, and within an hour, she could no longer see the coastline. She didn't feel sick. There were too many distractions. Anna stood at the rail and stared over the water. She studied the colours and reflections of the sky against the water and watched fish pass below the boat. She could see as far as the horizon, and there was not a cloud in the sky or a structure to spoil the view. It only took Anna a short while to fall in love with the sea. In an instant, Anna knew what she wanted out of life. She wanted space, and she wanted freedom. She loved the smell of the ocean, the fresh air, and the anticipation of going somewhere that she had never been before.

A young man with a flat cap stood a few yards from Anna. He couldn't have been much older than her. He had a shock of dark hair that tumbled out from under his cap, a broad smile and jet black eyes that smiled all the time.

The chap could see the joy on Anna's face as she stood at the rail.

"Isn't it magnificent?" he shouted out to her.

Anna laughed. Her smile was delightful, and she had perfect white teeth. Her eyes were almost closed against the bright light, and the sun caught the high-lights in her hair. The pale skin of her neck was perfect, but it was the laugh that caught Andrew off-guard. A joyous gurgle, it rose from her chest and es-caped onto the breeze. It was contagious, and soon he found himself chuckling too.

"What is your name?" she called out.

The young man walked over and stood next to her.

"Andrew Keegan."

"And who am I speaking to?"

A broad smile flooded his face.

"Anna."

"You've never been on a ship before?"

"No. How did you guess?"

"You look the way I felt the first time I sailed, only that I was five years old. I still feel that way now, mind you."

Anna laughed.

"I feel so free. I love the smell of the fresh sea air and the space. I feel—alive."

"It does that to you."

Andrew smiled at her.

"Are you a sailor?"

"Close, but no," he said in his lilting Irish accent.

Anna frowned and tilted her head to one side. Andrew laughed gently at her puzzled face.

"My father builds ships in Belfast. We have always lived close to the water. I sail as much as I can, but only for pleasure."

"Are you on your way to visit your family?"

"No. I am going back to a different grindstone," he chuckled.

"How so?"

"I am studying at Trinity College."

Anna nodded but felt intimidated by his status and education. She managed to hide it. This bright, happy, open young man was as refreshing as the sea air.

"And you, Anna, why are you travelling to Ireland?"

"I am going to look after my sick aunt," she lied.

Immediately, she was sorry for what she had done. Andrew seemed so sincere. He looked down at her belly.

"I am sorry to ask, but is it dangerous to be on a ship in your condition?"

"Oh yes, er, that," she muttered and looked down at her stomach.

For a moment, she had forgotten everything about her life in Salford and chatted to him as if she was a normal young girl with no complications.

"I am so sorry," said Andrew, looking down at the deck, embarrassed.

"Not to worry," she said, forcing a smile.

There was a strained silence between them. Andrew gave a nervous cough before attempting to break the ice for a second time.

"I brought some food with me for the journey. Would you like to share?"

"Oh, yes, please, I didn't think to pack in anything to eat."

"That's no good. There is still a long journey ahead of us before we reach Ireland."

'Us' thought Anna. It sounded so natural.

Andrew pulled a tin out of his bag. He opened it and passed her a piece of bread spread thick with salty butter and creamy yellow cheese. Anna took a bite and was convinced it was the best meal she had ever eaten.

"You are starving, aren't you," observed Andrew. "Come now, take another one. There's plenty."

Anna laughed.

"Well, that's good then. I haven't eaten since I arrived in Liverpool last night."

Andrew and Anna sat on a rickety bench and ate together in comfortable silence.

"It must be freezing out here in the winter," remarked Anna after she swallowed the last tasty bite.

"It is," agreed Andrew. "Ice hangs from the railings, and if you touch it with your bare hands, you stick to it. The sea is wild and thundering. The wind stings one's face, and you dare not remove your gloves for a minute."

Anna listened intently, absorbing everything that Andrew told her and demanding every detail.

> "I love it," said Andrew. "I love every moment on the ocean. I am studying to be an engineer. My father wants me to join the family business, but I would rather work on a ship for a few years and travel the world first before I get stuck in Belfast rattling round a drawing office or shipyard."
>
> "Don't you become afraid of drowning or freezing to death?"
>
> "Not really," he told her between taking bites out of his apple. "If you were on a boat with me, you would never get cold. I would wrap you up in a fur-lined oilskin coat that almost reached your toes and put thick woollen socks on your feet and padded leather gloves. You would never get cold. I would take care of that."

They finished the impromptu picnic. Andrew put his hand into his bag and pulled out a small flask with whiskey inside it.

> "Would you like a sip?" he offered. "It will warm you up."

Anna took a small sip, and he was right. She felt the warmth of the whiskey from her mouth to her stomach. She was convinced it warmed her to her ankles.

Andrew took two swigs and shoved the flask back into his bag.

They stood at the railing until sunset. The sea was dead calm. The sun sank closer to the horizon, and the sky turned from blue to green, then orange. Anna had never witnessed a proper sunrise or sunset. Nobody in Angel Meadows ever saw the heavens since it was permanently covered by a thick grey cloud, comprised of soot, coal dust and the black stink generated by the hordes of belching factories.

The orange glow on the horizon diminished until it became a thin orange line of fire that dimmed and eventually died.

"Just wait for a little." said Andrew, "there is another surprise coming."

A quarter moon rose over the horizon.

"Look there, Anna, behind you."

The sky turned as black as pitch. The sliver of the moon made no impact against the black heavens. Anna could hardly see her hand before her eyes. Slowly pinpricks of light became visible in the black sky. They became brighter and brighter until the majesty of a billion stars congested the night sky. It was the first time that Anna saw the Milky Way.

"Let us find a bench to sit on," Andrew said.

"I don't want to leave."

"We have to sit on deck, Anna, so you will still be able to see them."

With reluctance, Anna moved away from the rail.

"They're going to be out all night, Anna. They may seem to move around a bit, but you'll still see everything. I promise," Andrew added with a chuckle.

Andrew didn't ask Anna where she came from. He deduced from the awe for her surroundings that she had grown up in a very dark place. They sat down on a steel bench and would reach Dublin by morning.

Andrew was glad that he was travelling to Dublin. He hated the trips over to Liverpool. The experiences were always horrendous. The decks were over-loaded with the poorest of the poor hoping for a better future in England. Many of them were sick and exhausted from travelling for days or weeks. What disgusted Andrew the most was that it was the rule that the livestock travel below deck. The animals were valuable and had to reach their destination safely, the people less so. The frail men, women and children were left to the elements, some freezing to death, never reaching the paradise they envisaged England to be. The Irish emigrants were of no value. There were too many of them. They could be sacri-ficed.

Ireland had still not recovered from the Great Hun-ger. Andrew's grandfather, Matthew Keegan, was a hardworking man who had taken every opportunity he got to work even if it only paid a few pence. He did every filthy, menial job that was offered to him. Everyone was desperate to earn a living during the famine. It was, without doubt, the darkest period of Ireland's recent history.

Matthew Keegan was an astute observer. He realised that the problem was not the lack of money but that there was nothing to buy. The markets were empty. There was nothing to eat. Matthew worked for a small company that shovelled human and animal excrement off the streets of Belfast. Soon, he was promoted, and he would travel by cart and deliver the product to the farmers who used it as compost. On the way home, he would stop at all the peasants' cottages and allow them to scrape the dregs off the bottom of the cart. Some of the subsistence growers had very successful farms, so he purchased their excess fruit and vegetables and sold them at the Belfast market. Soon, he had a thriving business.

Grandma Keegan ran the market stall, and Matthew built the business. Grandpa Matthew was constantly at odds with the government or the church. Greed abounded, and the two mighty institutions were losing taxes and tithes because Matthew gave a lot of his money directly to the poor.

Matthew began supplying fresh produce to foreign ships, then he employed stevedores and finally became one of the biggest chandlers in Belfast. He realised that if he could do this in Belfast, he could do it anywhere in Ireland. But Grandpa Matthew showed his true colours when he realised that he could ship waste out of the city and dump it in the ocean.

A proud Emerald Islander, he refused to buy a boat from an Englishman. He had a hatred for English politicians that would never wane, and this hatred would fester in Keegan blood, from generation to generation. The boats that he could afford locally were rust buckets. Matthew Keegan was glum, but not for long. He examined the situation, pondered his options, and decided to build his own boat.

> The vessel was unique and somewhat unorthodox. He employed engineers to build the boilers and engines, and within no time, he had a small steam-driven boat that he called *'The Frances Keegan"*, after his wife.
>
> "It's temperamental," Grandpa told his mates, "just like Frances."

Grandma Frances was not impressed. She accused him of making a fool out of her. The blasted thing was likely to sink.

But it didn't. The sturdy little boat bobbed about the wild ocean and always returned to port safely.

> "Bleedin' miracle," the old woman used to mutter after every journey.

Matthew Keegan began to receive orders for the small dependable boats. Within a few years, the demands grew, and so did the vessels. Grandpa Matthew's business evolved from boatbuilding to shipbuilding.

He canny fellow had the foresight to send his son John to the university to study engineering. Thankfully, John enjoyed his subject. John Keegan took over the family business on the afternoon that Grandpa Matthew died, the old man still at work, collapsing from a heart attack, dying on a wharf in Belfast Harbour.

Andrew knew that he'd enjoyed a privileged upbringing, and he didn't take it for granted. His father was a reasonable and fair man, but not much had changed since Grandpa Matthew's day. The church still demanded their tithe, the government demanded tax, and now trade unions were throwing a spanner in the works, fighting for the working man. Andrew had heard a new trade union had raised its head in Manchester. Its offices were at Salford Quays. Of late, it had surged in popularity, slowly gobbling up the smaller unions to swell its ranks. Estimates suggested that this new union already had fifty thousand members and was run by a man called Colin Wheeler, known to be charming but ruthless.

The ferry reached the docks of Dublin as the sun rose. The air was still, and the sky was beautiful. Andrew watched Anna. She must have been exhausted. She had not slept all night.

"How long will you be in Dublin?" Keegan asked her.

"Six months."

"That's a long time. Won't you be going back to your husband?" he asked, looking at the thin gold ring on her finger.

"My husband died," she answered quickly.

"I am sorry. And the baby? When is it due?"

"Soon," said Anna.

"May I take you for tea when you are settled?"

Anna blushed, not understanding why this young man was so kind to her.

"—I don't know."

"I understand," said Andrew, a note of disappointment in his voice.

"It's just that I can't make any promises, and I like to keep my word," she mumbled.

"Of course. Forgive me."

She smiled at him.

"I will be at Trinity College. If you need help, Anna, you can find me there easy enough."

"Thank you."

They walked down the gangplank together. Neither one spoke a word. As they reached the bottom, Anna tripped over a loose plank. Andrew grabbed her hand to stop her fall.

"Steady, now, girl."

Instinctively, he pulled her towards him. Anna could feel his warm, strong hand around hers and then his hand in the small of her back as he steered her to a cab.

"Here then, Anna, off you go then. It was nice meeting you."

His eyes smiled as much as his mouth.

"Thank you. For everything."

"My pleasure."

Andrew turned to the cab driver, noticing her give him a dazzling smile.

"This young lady is visiting her aunt. Please take her to the address that she gives you."

"Yes, Sir," chirped the cab driver.

Andrew watched the cab leave. It turned up a narrow alley that led toward the centre of Dublin.

"Where to, Ma'am?" called the driver.

"Please take me to the cleanest boarding house you know of."

"You're not going to your aunt then?" he quizzed.

"Not today."

"The best place to stay is Mrs O'Connor's."

"Thank you. Please, take me there."

They passed rows and rows of houses, similar to those in Manchester. The mean abodes were squashed together, and people had used every ingenious method they could imagine to insulate themselves from the elements. The cold and damp had permeated the buildings. They were covered in mildew and moss, and the wooden structures were warped and peeling.

The streets began to get wider as they moved further away from the factories. They travelled up a slight hill, leaving the rows behind them. Soon, the cab came to a halt in front of a white house, stood in the middle of a patch of emerald green grass. A low, ornate iron fence surrounded the property. Anna admired the small garden, which was cheerful with the fragrant blooms of all colours scattered around the tidy flower beds. It was far more than Anna had hoped for. The cab driver saw her in shock.

"Do not fret, lass. It's not too dear. Mrs O'Connor takes in boarders to keep the bills paid. Her husband died a few years ago, and this is how she gets by," he said kindly.

"Thank you."

"Come now, love. Let me help you with those bags. My name is Gus. I bring a lot of people here. Mrs O'Connor trusts me to only bring well-behaved clients."

Gus didn't stop talking as he carried his bags up the steps to the front door. Before they could knock, Mrs O'Connor opened the door.

"Who have you brought with you today, Gus?" she cried out in good cheer.

"I hope that you have a room available for this here, lass," answered Gus, with as much enthusiasm.

"Of course, I do. If not, I will make space," chuckled Mrs O'Connor.

"What's your name then?"

"Anna Errington."

"Well, Anna Errington, welcome to my home. Please call me Mrs O. That's what everyone calls me. Now, I have the perfect room for you. It's a front room and gets more light than the others. I can't promise you sunlight, no I can't, but I can promise you the prettiest room in the house."

Anna had never experienced so much sincere kindness, and she smiled gratefully. The worries she had about travelling to Ireland alone were abating. The woman was cheerful and house proud, the perfect host. Anna looked about her. There was no display of wealth, but everything was well cared for. Mrs O led Anna upstairs and showed her to her room, lovely, small, and cosy.

"I made the quilt myself," said Mrs O proudly.

"It's beautiful."

"I got my friends to hunt me down bits and pieces, and I patched it all together."

Somehow Mrs O had created a work of art out of old scraps. She had managed to sew together the brightest, most cheerful quilt, an absolute reflection of her personality.

"Now then, Anna, you settle in. Then, when you are ready, come down to the kitchen."

Anna unpacked her suitcase and put her clothes into the chest of drawers and her dresses in a narrow cupboard. She had experienced Irish hospitality since she boarded the ferry in Liverpool.

Alas, for all this kindness, Anna was depressed. Inevitably, the thought of returning to drab Manchester and her marriage of convenience already felt like returning to captivity. She didn't miss her loud, charismatic husband and his political cronies. She didn't miss their shabby house in Salford.

Anna Errington didn't want wealth or power. Above everything else, she wanted freedom.

8

MARRIAGE AND MISERY

Mary Riddle found a small apartment in Manchester near the university, and Alec found new chambers in the centre of the city. The young girl was wholly engrossed in her subject matter. Alec had to coax her away from her books to receive any attention. It intrigued him that this slip of a girl, from one of the worst hell holes in the world, had been born with such a superior intellect.

Mary ignored her fellow students, who often wondered who she was and where she came from. When the exam results were published on the law faculty noticeboard, her name always topped the list. She avoided her professors and only communicated with them in writing. Her questions were complex and stymied her seniors. Mary was an enigma to the others, mysterious and almost invisible.

For the first time in many years, Alec was happy. He had never ever told Mary about his occasional dissatisfactions with their relationship. He had always accepted a life on her terms, and they had lived that way for years. One thing did trouble him—the late discovery of her real her age. The idea of sleeping with a fourteen-year-old had disturbed him ever since. By the time he realised his folly, his options were few. He had become fond of the young woman, but she was a legal risk. He considered ending the relationship. Each time he felt bold enough to end the relationship, his courage failed him. Finally, he realised that he didn't want to lose her and couldn't let her go and began the mental countdown for her to reach the age of consent.

The small business that he had formed in Manchester was becoming successful, and soon he had a sea of clients who came to see him. He was a fine solicitor and developed an excellent reputation. Mary often helped him in his research. Soon, she was helping him with as many cases as she could. Some were highly complex, others were simple, but he always admired her interpretation of the rule of law and how she applied it rigorously no matter the gravity of the case.

Alec was a proud and competitive man. He knew that Mary would study as a barrister and would not settle for anything less than excellence. As much as he loved and respected his wife, he would not kowtow to her academically, and he enrolled himself to study as well. The atmosphere in their home was tense but driven. They spent nights studying and rushed between the office and the university during the day to see their clients. Desperate to maintain order, they hired Miss Rowena Jenkins.

Their lives were on a steady track, soon to be complicated by an unexpected but overdue event. Mary discovered that she was pregnant. She accepted the information in her customary cool, aloof manner and withheld the information from her husband until she had carefully weighed her options. As always, Mary was distant and enigmatic.

She broke the news to Alec over dinner.

"I'm pregnant," said Mary.

Alec's face lit up. He stood up in excitement, wanting to run toward her and embrace her.

"Do not get up," she ordered as Alec looked at her, confused.

"I will have a procedure. I don't want the child."

Alec felt as if someone had knocked the wind out of him. For a moment, he found it difficult to breathe as he sat at the head of the table, bewildered.

"Why?"

"I told you I would not have a child," Mary said calmly.

"But it will make me happy," said her husband.

"We have an agreement."

"But it's illegal, Mary?"

"It's non-negotiable."

Alec didn't go to their bedroom that night. He poured himself drink after drink to ease his pain. He stumbled into their room at sunrise and sat next to her on the bed.

"Please, Mary," he begged, "please, don't do it."

Mary ignored him.

"Make me a cup of tea, will you? I have a busy day ahead."

She had every intention of aborting the child. She read up the law on abortions which loosely interpreted said that it was illegal and both patient and doctor would go to gaol. Mary was meticulous. She had no intention of going to gaol.

At breakfast, Mary made an excuse that she had to go to the Liverpool Library.

She travelled by train and found a room for the night in the slums. She reasoned that many women in the family way chose to end their pregnancies, especially among the poor. It would be the ideal place to find someone to conduct the procedure.

Mary dressed in black and set off to find a doctor. She refused to give birth to a child for whom she had no feelings. She was doing this for the only person who mattered in her life, herself.

A tall man with spectacles greeted Mary. The waiting room was cold, there was a mean fire behind the brass grate, but it made no difference to the air temperature. The reception room was empty, and she was relieved that no one could testify to seeing her there. She was not ashamed of what she was about to do. Rather, she cared that she would ruin her reputation as a barrister. Mary was loathing to allow this quick operation to destroy her opportunity of becoming a successful, wealthy woman.

The man with the glasses called out her name in an official voice.

"Mrs Dawn Browning?"

Mary stood up and walked across the black-and-white tiled floor. The man with the spectacles opened the door and motioned for her to enter. As she walked toward the desk, her eyes scanned the room in a single glance. It was tatty, and the doctor had dirty nails. She sat down opposite the doctor, her posture perfect, her clothing immaculate.

Doctor Wyatt delighted in humbling patients. He summed up their situation in a trice. Mary sensed he was not a man to cross. Still, she didn't need to like him. She was there for a purpose. All she had to do was tolerate him as he supplied a service.

Mary was candid about the situation. The doctor was puzzled by her matter of fact demeanour. Usually, patients gave him cryptic clues to their condition, and he would have to guess the ailment by process of elimination.

"I am pregnant. I have no desire to have a child. I need you to arrange to dispose of it."

The doctor was surprised at the stark comment. Most women would be tearful by now and begging his silence. Mrs Browning showed no emotion whatsoever. It was clear she had made a was a coldly calculated decision.

"What does your husband say about the situation, Mrs Browning? Is he in agreement with your decision?"

"I have not discussed it with him," said Mary. "I don't believe that it's any of his business."

Wyatt frowned.

"But, Mrs Browning, it is his child. He has the right to know your intentions."

"I have no intention of justifying myself to you."

"I am only saying," tutted the doctor. "Surely, he should have a say in what happens next?"

"Do you force these questions upon the working-class women who come to you? Or are you satisfied to ask an exorbitant fee for a safe procedure and keep your opinions to yourself?"

The physician clenched his jaw in anger. His patients never answered him back.

"I am sure that Mr Browning would not be satisfied to sacrifice a son," the doctor responded, annoyed.

"I repeat—it is none of your business."

Wyatt tried to hide his astonishment, keeping his eyes fixed on the ice-cold face of the woman in front of him.

"What does your husband do for a living?"

Mary ignored the question.

"I would like to get on with the business of terminating this pregnancy."

Mary studied him coolly, noticing he was struggling to deal with the hard woman in front of him.

"I don't do this work myself. I will send you to another doctor. It will cost you a lot of money. The doctor I am suggesting is more of your social status. His fee is hefty. He works from a house on the outskirts of the city. It is clean. If you want to pay less, you will have to see someone in the slums, but there is no guarantee of your survival."

"Is this doctor well-educated?"

"Oxford. He knows what he is doing, and seventy-five per cent of his patients survive."

"Is that all? What does he do with the corpses of the women he kills?"

Dr Wyatt shrugged, and it made him look stupid.

"Is he discreet?"

"Yes, he only takes care of women of a certain social class. He can have his license revoked if anyone finds out about his—uhm—extra-curricular activities. It's illegal," muttered the man.

"What are you going to charge me?" asked the ever-logical Mary.

"For a woman of your stature, the price is £100. As you can understand, this matter must be kept confidential. I am sure that you are prepared to pay for discretion, Mrs

> Browning. You don't need this episode to pop up awkwardly in the future, do you?"
>
> "That sounds like blackmail, Dr Wyatt," she snapped.

For the first time, the doctor felt that he was in control of the situation. Her snippiness had betrayed her outward candour. He had driven the point home, got the upper hand. Her secret would not be safe if she didn't pay up.

Dr Wyatt thought that he had won. Now, all the desperate woman had to do was capitulate and accept his terms.

> "I have faced worse men than you, Dr Wyatt," said Mary. "Until now, nothing about you has impressed me. You are cheap and dirty, and I don't take threats lightly."

She looked him straight in the eye, doubting that the fee was honest. Wyatt sat back in his chair and watched her. He truly believed that she was having a moral and ethical struggle, when in fact, she was having neither. Mary was cunning and shrewd. She weighed up which choice would be the best for her.

> "Dr Wyatt, I have thought about this very seriously. The solution you are supplying is unsatisfactory. From the moment I walked into this room, you have been smug and arrogant. You have taken it for granted that I

will trade on your terms. You have exploited my status, and you've made a grave mistake."

"I have asked you if you're going to use my practice. I didn't ask you your opinion."

"No, Dr Wyatt. I am not going to use your practice. Neither am I going to destroy your practice—today. But if you ever threaten to blackmail me or discuss this visit with anyone, I assure you that I will have you killed."

Mary looked at the man coldly. Her eyes were two tiny beads of blue ice. Her hooked nose and thin lips reminded Dr Wyatt of a hawk. He was terrified. He knew from the look in her eyes that she would do exactly as she said. He stopped behaving with an arrogant demeanour. He ceased to feel superior. He would never ever say a word about this woman to anyone, nor would he ever cross her path. For as long as he lived, he prayed that she would never come to see him again.

Mary left the surgery and walked towards the library. She had already forgotten about Dr Wyatt.

Back in Manchester, Alec was hiding behind a wall of silence. He sat in his chair and stared out of the window for hours. He didn't know what Mary was feeling or thinking—or doing, for that matter. He only knew was that he had promised her that she could make her own decisions about her life, body, soul, and business. Alec was an honourable man, and he would leave her to take whichever course of action she chose.

Mary found the house on the outskirts of Liverpool. An old woman opened the door and admitted her discreetly. The woman asked her for payment, and Mary gave her the money. There was no receipt. She went into a clean room and was told to remove her underwear and lie on a gurney-like bed.

The doctor came into the room. He was clean and well-spoken. He didn't bother to introduce himself or ask her name. In his experience, all the women lied to him.

"If you die," he began.

"I have no intention of dying," said Mary.

"Very good."

The doctor didn't say another word. His approach was professional, and his technique flawless. Mary didn't flinch or show fear. The doctor thought it was quite unusual.

"You will remain here for several hours. The foetus has to wash out."

Mary nodded but said nothing.

The woman showed Mary to a room and insisted that she lay on a bed. Within a short while, Mary started to experience cramps and then began to bleed. The old woman stood between her legs as the child left Mary's body.

"It's all done then. You can go home shortly."

"I want to see it."

"What?"

"I want to see it."

The old woman was shocked. She had never had that request before. Most women were terrified and emotional by now. She fetched a small enamel dish, and Mary looked at it. The foetus was the same shape and size as a sheep's kidney. It had two black dots for eyes and stubby arms and legs.

"That thing is disgusting," said Mary. I can't believe it was in my body.

Mary dressed, feeling fine. The item on her to-do list had gone well.

"Give the doctor a message from me," Mary ordered.

"Yes?"

"Tell him he is risking his life if he discusses my visit with anybody."

Mary began walking toward the front door. She turned around and stared straight into the woman's eyes:

"—And that goes for you as well."

Mary walked down the street. By the time she reached the corner, she had already forgotten the procedure and the thing in the dish.

She hailed a cab driver.

"Where to Ma'am?"

"The university, I have work to do."

9

THE JOURNEY

There was a bold knock, and it startled Mrs O'Connor. The cheerful little Irish woman dashed to the front door and peered through the stained-glass panes to see who was making the racket. She stared into the face of a good-looking gentleman with a bright smile.

"And who are you, if I may ask?" she said without a 'hello' or 'good afternoon'.

She had a big smile, and Andrew Keegan laughed.

"I am here to visit Anna," he said with a wide grin.

"Oh dear, she didn't tell me that she was expecting anyone as handsome as you," said Mrs O Connor with a twinkle in her eye.

Andrew studied the little woman closely. He was trying to decide if she was nosey or sincere. Andrew gave her the benefit of the doubt. Surely, someone that happy was a godsend in these dark days.

"Let me call her," smiled Mrs O'Connor. "She's out in the kitchen helping us bake bread. Does she know who you are?"

"Of course, she knows who I am. We travelled from Liverpool to Dublin on the ferry."

"Good, then come in and take a seat in the parlour. There you go. Sit down on that chair and get comfortable."

Andrew obeyed the cheerful bossy little woman.

"How about a nice cup of tea?"

Andrew smiled and nodded. He was delighted that Mrs O'Connor was prepared to have him visit for a while yet. The woman went into the kitchen and looked up the stairs.

"Anna," she shouted at the top of her lungs, "you've got a visitor. Some sailor you met on the ferry on the way here."

Anna's head appeared, and she looked at Mrs O'Connor, wondering which sailor could be looking for her.

"I don't know any sailors," answered Anna. "Surely, he has the wrong address."

"Well, there's a young man in the parlour who says that he met you on the ferry from Liverpool to Dublin."

Anna put back ahead and laughed.

"Oh yes," she said, "you talking about Andrew Keegan. He looked after me very well while we did the crossing, but I wonder how he found me."

"Aww, I bet it was Gus and his big old mouth," shouted Mrs O'Connor loud enough for the neighbours to hear. "Well, go ahead then, lass, go and say hello. I will bring you some tea and something to eat while the two of you have a jolly old chinwag."

Anna walked down the narrow hall and into the parlour. Andrew Keegan looked a lot less windblown than when she had first seen him on the ship. He was all scrubbed up, looking as handsome as ever."

"Hello, Anna."

There was no tension in his voice.

"Andrew!" she exclaimed. "How on earth did you find me?"

She smiled from ear to ear.

"It wasn't much of a job. I put you in Gus's cab. He's well-known in Dublin, so I tracked him down, and he told me that he had brought you up here. I was thrilled to hear that because Mrs O'Connor certainly runs a good boarding house. It's clean, and as you can see it in a lovely area."

"That's true," said Mary. "I am enjoying every single moment of being here. Mrs O'Connor has been so good to me."

Andrew Keegan looked at her. The baby had grown significantly over the last few weeks. He was reluctant to ask too many questions about the bump. He didn't want to upset her as he had on the ferry. It was none of his business.

"Not to worry," she laughed when she saw him glance at her stomach.

He didn't say anything.

"You are trying to guess when the baby is coming. It is due any day now. Mrs O'Connor has arranged a midwife to help me. I am a bit terrified. I hope everything goes well—"

She broke off, remembering that women weren't to discuss these things with men.

"There are thousands of people on the earth," said Andrew. "It has to be successful. Mother Nature knows a thing about it too."

Anna burst out laughing. Mrs O'Connor arrived with a tray of eats and put them on the table in front of them.

"Thank you, Mrs O'Connor," said Andrew and Anna simultaneously.

"It's a pleasure, my loves," she said. "Let me leave you in peace. You probably have a lot to talk about."

She closed the door behind her after taking a good look at Anna and Andrew, soaking up every nuance. They would make a handsome couple, and she could see that the young man really liked Anna, and Anna liked him too. Mrs O'Connor was a hopeless romantic and began working on a plan to have them see each other more often.

Anna watched Andrew as he poured out his tea.

"What have you been doing while you have been here, Anna? Seen much of the city?"

"No. Mostly, I've been helping around the house. I can't sit still for a moment, and it's been wonderful to be of use to Mrs O'Connor. She only has two people working for her, so she is very grateful for their help."

Andrew frowned. Mary looked at him, uncertain of what he was thinking. Finally, Andrew spoke.

> "I don't want to—I don't mean to mind your business, Anna," he said gently, "but I need to understand something. When you spoke to me on the ship, you said you were coming to take care of your aunt. How did you end up at Mrs O'Connor?"

Anna blushed. She had forgotten the lie she had told Andrew. She didn't know what to say or do.

Anna looked down at the floor, ashamed of herself and embarrassed.

> "I am sorry," said Andrew. "I shouldn't have asked you that question. It was rude and embarrassing."

Anna smiled, but it was not a sincere smile. She was struggling to keep up the pretence of being happy. She was struggling to accept that she had lied, especially to such a nice person

> "You can tell me anything, Anna. We are friends. I am not going to judge you. I am sure there is a very good reason to hide the truth, and I accept it. If you can't tell me, that's fine. I'll still be your friend."

He smiled kindly.

Anna couldn't return the smile. She had to decide. She could tell him the truth, or she could lie again. She decided that the truth was so much easier and less complicated.

"I am married to a man called Colin Wheeler in Manchester."

"Colin Wheeler, the union leader?"

"Yes," replied Anna. "This is not my husband's child. Unfortunately, I had an affair with another man who refused to marry me, and Colin was kind enough to propose, and, well, I accepted. My child's life would have been hell on earth otherwise."

Anna held her breath. This was not the kind of information that you easily shared with someone else, especially a man. It would be completely shocking to anyone who had grown up with any form of morality or ethics. She was a fallen woman. These scenarios were common in Angel Meadows. It happened to so many girls. It was usually a three-day wonder within the community until the next girl fell. The community would hide their sordid underbelly to the best of their ability when outsiders interfered. There was a powerful tribalism in Angel Meadows, while all the different factions within its boundaries could be critical and cruel to each other, no outsider had the privilege to do the same.

Andrew looked serious. She was sure that he was disgusted by her.

"I am sure you're not the first or the last girl that this has happened to."

Anna couldn't believe what she was hearing

> "I am not an old man, you know. I am born in a more modern age. I don't believe in harsh judgement for women. We never know what circumstances lead to the pregnancy. I've got a mother, sisters, and aunts. We weren't always a rich family. There's a great history of normalcy in our family," Andrew laughed. "My father taught me not to judge. Besides, Colin accepted you, warts and all."

Anna was sorry that she had to hear Colin's name come into the conversation.

> "I am not in love with Colin," Anna confessed. "But, I am lucky that he is a good man to me."

As Andrew watched her, he reflected that she was very easy to love.

> "Do you want to go back to England, Anna?"

She was not expecting the question and kept quiet.

> "You see, Anna, if you want to stay in Ireland, I will do everything that I can to keep you here. My family will protect you."
>
> "How do you know they will?"
>
> "I told my father about you."

Anna took a deep breath. For the first time in her life, she had the power to decide for herself.

"I don't believe that you should live with a man that you don't love," he reassured.

"And how many times have you been in love, Andrew?"

"Oh, now you're talking," laughed Andrew. "I fell in love with all my sisters' friends, but I was made way too much of a man to write poems and love letters. So, the poor girl never ever knew. Then I would try to hold their hand, and they would run away."

Andrew had a way of lightening the mood, and soon Anna was laughing again.

"The experience taught me a few things. I realised very early that if you care for someone, you have to make it clear from the beginning."

"Ah. So, you are an expert."

"Anna, I don't know you at all, but I know that we are going to be very firm friends for the rest of our lives. I would like to be part of your future."

Anna could believe what she heard. She was not sure if it was a statement of love or just one of a friendship.

"What about the baby?" she asked him.

"She is going to be as beautiful as her mother."

He smiled broadly.

"And how do you know it's a girl?"

"I've always been right with my sisters."

"Really?"

"Yes, I am a fortune-teller as well," Andrew laughed. "We could live in a caravan, and I can make money telling fortunes. We will have a wonderful income."

The mood changed.

"I am sorry, Andrew, but I am going to be forced to go back to my husband. Everyone in Manchester knows that I am married to him. Sooner or later, the union will open an office in Dublin or Belfast. He is much older than me, and he is also becoming more and more powerful. He will never tolerate that that I embarrass him. Your family has offices in Belfast and Dublin. He and your father are bound to cross paths somewhere. I understand that you mean this kindly—"

"—you will be happier here. We will arrange for you to divorce him, or I will pay him a hefty sum to divorce you."

"I would be happy to stay and begin a new life and pretend to be a widow, but be assured, someone will recognise me, and it will cause your family embarrassment. I have caused enough trouble for everyone around me already—and I don't want that for you."

Andrew nodded looked a little sad.

"Well, even if you're not prepared to move to Ireland, do you mind if we stay friends? I will visit you from time to time. I am sure Mrs O'Connor will make a fine chaperone."

"Yes," agreed Anna, "I think that would be lovely."

"How long are you planning to stay here after you've had the baby?"

Anna didn't find it difficult to be honest with him. He was so easy to speak to, and his cheerful non-judgmental attitude was a breath of fresh air.

"I have to remain here for three months after the baby is born. There are always people who will count the days and months, so we have decided that I will return to Manchester when the child is three months old. We will register its birth date in England."

Andrew had spent quite a few hours with Anna, and finally, it was time to leave.

"Thank you for visiting me," she said. "I enjoyed seeing you."

"I am glad to be friends, Anna."

"Me too."

Mrs O'Connor peeped at them from the kitchen door. Anna opened the door for Andrew, and as he stepped past her, he bent over and kissed her on the cheek. The nosey landlady couldn't hold her excitement, and by the time Anna stepped into the kitchen, everyone knew that Andrew had kissed her.

While Anna was preparing for motherhood and filled with anxiety about the birth, Colin Wheeler was having a grand old time back in Salford. The relationship between Anna and Colin was complex. He wasn't the father of the child, so he didn't have a responsibility toward it, other than a roof over its head and food in its belly. Once this dawned upon him, he began to question his loyalty to Anna.

He had moved the club to better premises, and doing so, his head swelled to even greater proportions. He took on the persona of a king and bossed everyone around him. He demanded they meet all his orders, no matter how ridiculous they were.

He had taken to spending time with Shady. He kept it a secret from his friends, but all the servants knew she was coming to the house late at night and leaving in the early hours of the morning. Colin knew that it would not do his career any good if news of these illicit liaisons leaked out. Shady had a good business, but she was tired and afraid of losing her looks and felt she needed to change her lifestyle, maybe calm down a bit. But when push came to shove, hedonistic Colin wanted to continue his escapades, whatever the risk to his public image. She satisfied him more than any other woman he had met. He learned that the working class had never been too worried about morals and were open to his more exotic predilections.

Despite the distractions, Colin managed to maintain his loyal following. But Colin was developing a taste for force and violence. It was an expedient route to obedience. He had opposition, and his charm was no longer as effective as it used to be.

Colins's comeuppance arrived in a most unusual way. He had made it clear that he would destroy the Perreira family if they dared to cross his path or interfere with his marriage to Anna. This reached the ears of the fierce and proud Perreira clan, and the family refused to tolerate a mere stranger who threatened their livelihood.

Yes, the Perreira family was delighted Colin had married Anna. It meant that they were spared the shame and embarrassment of Mario's virility, tarnishing them forever. By now, Mario was happily married and far happier than he could ever have imagined. His loyal wife was pregnant, and at the size of her belly, everybody was convinced that she would give birth to twins. Even though this had nothing to do with Marco's performance, he took all credit for being able to create two babies instead of one. Mario's wife was a typical Mediterranean woman who served her husband unconditionally. She had set up a typical Portuguese family home, she was the matriarch, but he had the final word. He had observed this in his parent's marriage. His foreboding Mama always got her way. The hierarchy in the relationship appealed to Mario because it gave him the opportunity to be lazy yet also selfish and self-serving. As was fit for a wife, the pregnant Sofia would stay at home while he would gallivant. Either he would spend nights drinking and gambling or making endless love to some tart who was only too happy to service the good-looking young man, a far cry from their regular flabby, florid clientele. There was an endless battle between the prostitutes as to who would have the honour of the young Adonis's body.

It was mid-morning when Mario arrived at work. His father was livid by his tardiness, but he had greater problems to discuss with his wayward son.

"Why are you so late?" demanded his father.

"I was out last night. I got home just before sunrise."

"I don't mind you having fun, Mario, but I suggest that you get to work on time. This is where you earn your bread and butter. You wouldn't be able to spend anything on any of those wenches if you had no money. You are a prosperous man, remember where your money comes from, and show some respect?"

Mario didn't say anything. His father seldom became angry with him, which led Mario to believe that there was a different reason for his father's wrath.

"Some news has reached my ears," said the old man.

Mario lifted his groggy head.

"What is it, Papa? What have you heard?"

"Wheeler has sent us a message via one of his henchmen. He will burn down our store if anyone finds out about the true father of Anna's child."

Marcus looked at his father, hardly understanding. What the old man was saying? Surely the matter was in the past?

"Colin Wheeler has a vendetta against us. I don't take to this lightly. No man is going to burn down my business," Mr Perreira raged in Portuguese.

"Nobody will touch anything that your Mama and I have built up in this country. Our family doesn't go around threatening anybody else.

We must find a way to take care of the situation."

Mario felt ashamed. He was responsible for the situation. Even if he was poor marriage material and a spoilt brat, Mario still felt a fierce loyalty and love for his family. He would never be able to live with himself if anything happened to his father. Mr Perreira had sweated and slaved to start his business. He ran an honest, simple business—well, mostly honest, barring a few incidents where he cheated the tax man out of a few bob.

"I expect you to do something about this, my son. I thought this sorry situation was behind us, but it seems it is not. Mario, you have caused this shameful situation. You have led us into dangerous territory."

"Yes, Papa," said Mario, unable to look his father in the eye.

Once Mr Perreira started, he couldn't stop. It was as if the years of cuckolded frustration that had built up in him had finally culminated into one catastrophic explosion.

"For the first time in my life," said Papa Perreira, "I want to leave your Mama. There is not one night that goes by when she spends hours complaining about you. She continually curses that girl you got pregnant. Tells me to do something about it. Now this threat from Wheeler has tipped her over the edge.

She's ruining my life. Her raging loose tongue will cause us problems. Do you understand me? If this doesn't come to an end. I am going to pack my bags and go back to the old country by myself. I refuse to spend my last years with a cantankerous woman who's driving me mad, dodging an army of union men who want to slit my throat."

"Yes, Papa." said Mario, "I will take care of Wheeler."

"I don't care how you do it. I don't mind if you've got a whore every night. Just take some responsibility. Calm your mother down. And make sure we don't lose our business, or you will not be my son."

Mario spent a few days thinking about how he would take care of the situation. He hated Colin Wheeler. Even though the man seemed He and friendly, Mario knew that he was dangerous and untrustworthy.

Mario was mildly relieved when Colin decided to marry Anna. Word on the street was that the union man was in a relationship with Shady and that he had only married Anna as a smokescreen to make himself look squeaky clean.

There was another reason Wheeler needed pulling down a peg or two. Mario would never forgive Colin Wheeler for humiliating him by pursuing Anna in public and stealing her from under his nose. It turned out that Mario was delighted for the opportunity at revenge.

He might have been spoilt, but he was not stupid. He was as shrewd as anybody else who had to survive in Salford. His father watched him constantly, wondering what his son's next move would be—and when. Papa Perreira was a patient man, but he would only give his son a week to find a solution. Within a few days, Mario knew what he would do.

It was a dismal afternoon in Salford, and Mario took a casual stroll to the dockyard. He found he found the New St George's Club, as Colin had called it. It was just a tad cleaner than the original St George that had been above the old laundry. It was Friday, and he knew that Colin would be there. He was standing at the bar counter, in the throes of giving a political speech. The man was never happier than when he was the centre of the universe.

As Mario had predicted, Colin's all-knowledgeable booming voice was the first thing he heard when he entered the club. The new arrival stood in the background, watching Colin dominating the room while both women and men hung on his every word. A far as Mario was concerned, it was all a lot of rubbish. Many people who worked for the Perreiras wanted to join the growing union, but Papa told them in no uncertain terms that if they joined Colin Wheeler, they would be fired on the spot.

> "I will not have my staff dictating the terms
> and conditions of their employment to me,"
> the old grocer would yell.

Colin was annoyed to see the belligerent young man and was surprised that he had the gall to show up at the club. Did the threat to the Perreira family mean nothing? Mario was not a union man, and it irked Wheeler. His attendance would raise eyebrows, and that was the last thing Colin wanted to happen.

Wheeler rushed through his rhetoric, eager to know what Mario was doing there. He approached his nemesis with gusto. The outsider had placed himself in a corner of the room where he could see everything. He wanted to see where all Colin's cronies were standing in case he needed to escape the room in a hurry. He didn't know how far Colin would go to have him gone.

> "And what are you doing here, young Mario?"
> Colin asked sarcastically. "I thought you
> would be selling your cabbages at this time
> of the day. I hardly think this is an establishment that you should be visiting, given your
> criticism of our union."

Mario smiled and didn't say anything. Colin was not a man to stop goading once he had identified a weakness in someone.

> "Is your father's business still standing?"
> Colin asked facetiously. "If you are here to

cause trouble, your business may not be standing when you get back to it."

They were just the words that Mario was waiting for. And he turned his head and faced Colin.

"We need to talk about that," said Mario. "My brothers and cousins don't like your threats. Neither does my Papa."

"What do you think you're going to do about it?" Wheeler asked with a menace in his voice.

"I am going to tell everybody that Anna's child is illegitimate," answered Mario. "You will look like an idiot in front of everyone. You will be a joke. Your cosy career will be over, creaming all that money off, pretending to help. Desgraçados are two-a-penny in Salford. People will forget my family's shame a lot quicker than your greed and corruption, stealing off hard-working men to fund your lifestyle."

Colin had never faced such a vicious threat. He had never expected that Mario Perreira would have the gumption to respond to his threats or threaten to out his secret about the baby's parentage. Colin knew that he had been pushed into a corner, and being a politician, he had vulnerabilities. He decided to be quiet, then his pride got the better of him.

"I am not afraid of your little colony," Wheeler spat.

"It is not only the Portuguese who loathe your ego," Mario said coolly, "the Irish and Jews are sick of you as well."

Colin tried to remain poker-faced, but this was very bad news. If he lost this support, he might as well retire. He realised that the young Mario had outplayed him. Life as he knew it may never be the same after this. Colin would need to take drastic measures to save his reputation.

Mario slammed his glass on the counter, and the liquid spilt. Colin looked at the mess Mario had left behind as he marched out of the club.

Wheeler had an inkling of a plan. The way to solve both their problems permanently was to get rid of Anna. Yes, that was the way forward.

Colin was cunning. He would expose Annie as a liar and harlot. It would show everybody that he was strong. He would expose the child she was having and deny his knowledge of her pregnancy. Then he would get Mary's note from the desk and expose that Bernard Errington was not her father. He would reinforce the betrayal by exposing that the despised Dickie Woods was her father. He would allow the press to publish all the distasteful details and ensure that it was splashed across the frontpage headlines.

Colin was not too concerned about Anna. He would divorce her. She would be ashamed and disappear. Young and beautiful and likely to end up in a brothel. After a few years, she would lose her looks, and who knew what would happen then. Besides, who cared? It was not his problem.

10

ELIZABETH

Anna's child what's born at two o'clock on a wet Thursday afternoon. The rain was coming down in torrents, beating a steady pace against the roof. Anna's labour was thirty minutes short of eighteen hours, and Mrs O'Connor was beside herself with concern. The midwife Mrs Tutton assured her that it was normal for a young woman to take longer having her first, but that had not been Mrs O'Connor's experience, and she was in a panic. Anna was a gentle soul, and she didn't anticipate the pain.

A little earlier at noon, someone walked up the path to the house. It was an unusual hour to have a visitor. Andrew Keegan was popping in for his regular chat. As he walked into the hallway, he could hear Anna's screams coming from upstairs. One of the servants let him in and made polite excuses. Mrs O'Conner came to see who it was.

"Oh, dear God," she cried. "I don't know what to do. It's far worse for her than I thought it would be. I must get back. You do understand—"

O'Conner dashed back, her skirts rustling as she ran, holding onto her bonnet. The screams were so loud and tortured that Andrew couldn't bear to hear them. He felt hopeless, overcome with compassion. Eventually, it became unbearable to sit in the parlour sipping tea and hear the pained yelping of his poor Anna. He stood up and headed for the staircase, bounding up them two steps at a time.

"Don't come in here," called Mrs O'Connor. "It's no place for a man."

Andrew Keegan couldn't withhold his tongue.

"I can't sit and drink blasted tea and pretend I can't hear her. I want to see her."

"No! Don't go in here."

Too late to stop him, he was already at the top of the staircase, pushing past her to get into the tiny room. The midwife was too busy to even notice him. Anna was lying on the bed with her nightclothes bunched up around her waist. Her legs were pulled up. She was writhing in pain, and perspiration drenched her beautiful face. When the midwife eventually raised her eyes and saw Andrew, it was too late to tell him to leave. He had already seen everything there was to see. Andrew went to the top of the bed. His only concern was Anna's comfort. He'd heard the women in his family talk about a myriad of births, and none of the women said they wanted to be left alone without a friend.

> "Look at me, Anna," Andrew said tenderly. "Look at me. I am here to help you."

Anna met his eyes. She was exhausted.

> "You don't have to do this alone."

He saw a flicker of light in her eyes.

> "Come now, sweetheart, I know that you can do this. You are going to make such a beautiful mother."

Andrew Keegan spoke in a tender Irish lilt, and the midwife got tears in her eyes. As he soothed her, The midwife proceeded to give Anna orders on how she could make things better for herself. She managed to calm herself down somewhat and began to follow the midwife's instructions step by step.

Keegan was devastated to watch the lovely girl in pain. Finally bearing down for the final push, Anna used all her strength and gave birth to a little girl. Then the midwife got the child to scream with a smack so hard it made the tot swing beneath her raised arm. Both Anna and Andrew got such a fright that they jumped.

"What a wonderful voice," said Andrew as the child bawled.

Anna smiled. It was an exhausted smile, but it was the most beautiful one that Andrew had ever seen. Anna held the child in her arms, and the girl began to suckle. The crinkled little face already had the features of her mother. Andrew instinctively knew that this little lass was going to be beautiful. He knew that she would have the same spirit and joy that attracted him to Anna on the ferry.

Mrs O'Connor didn't bother to give Andrew a talking to. It was far too late for that. He had calmed the situation, and she was grateful for that. Without his help, the situation would have been dire. She went to the kitchen to supervise the making of a suitably light meal. She sent the rich broth up to the new mother with a hot pot of tea. Anna and Andrew drank and ate. Mrs O'Connor held the bouncing baby.

"Oh, she is a beauty. She is going to be just like you, Anna."

"I can't see that," said Anna laughing. "She's all wrinkly."

"She's got your smile," gushed Andrew.

"What are we going to call her?" asked Mrs O'Connor as she cooed over the tot, rubbing noses.

"Her name will be Elizabeth," declared Andrew.

Both women looked at him.

"Why Elizabeth?" asked Anna.

"I think it is a fine name," he answered, "and she is truly a gift from God."

"Well Elizabeth," said Mrs O'Connor looking at the child, "welcome to the family."

Andrew soon became a regular visitor. How he managed to study and spend as much time with Anna and Elizabeth was a mystery. The new mother recovered quickly, and she was filled with joy every time she looked at her baby. Andrew was enchanted with both mother and daughter. He would watch, captivated by the way she displayed such open adoration for Elizabeth. She crept into Andrew's heart and made a home for herself there. Although it was taboo socially, Andrew would accompany them on walks through the park, and they would stop at little tea rooms and enjoying each other's company.

Andrew knew that he was in love with Anna. The instant he had seen her on the ferry, he felt attracted to her. That she was pregnant made no difference to him. But how did she feel? Andrew was finding it difficult to keep his feelings at bay. She would be leaving soon, and he had no right to expect anything from her. Marrying Wheeler meant she had a life back in Manchester to return to. He had extended the hand of friendship and made it clear that he was always there for her. He desired her, but even if she did offer him the pleasure of her body, he would resist because it would make it so much more difficult to let her go. He didn't want the pleasure of her for one night and then struggle through a painful goodbye. He wanted all of her every night for the rest of their lives.

The feeling was mutual for Anna, but she didn't dare consider a future with him. She had found someone with whom she could laugh. Her Irish family were sincere and generous. Above all, she felt safe. She didn't know how she would face filthy Salford and her bombastic husband, a man she didn't love. Although Andrew was a nice man, she would never fit into his world. She was a woman with a complicated past that would ruin Andrew's reputation. She would never feel good enough for him.

She made up her mind. She had no choice but to return to Colin. If she disappeared, his career would suffer. For everything that he had done for her, she owed him her loyalty. The guilt would follow her, poisoning any future chance of happiness.

Anna's last days in Dublin were like a fairy tale. The days were warm, and there was a hiatus in the rain. Andrew spent the days outside with her, enjoying the clear sky, surrounded by the greenest grass that God had created. Flowers popped up everywhere in the gardens and woods.

But it was all a fantasy that would end soon.

Gus drove Anna back to the ferry, Mrs O'Connor and Andrew keeping her company. They were all in tears as they said goodbye to each other. At first, Andrew was cordial, but when it was his turn to wish Anna good luck, he pulled her into his arms and held her tight.

> "I will never forget you, Anna. You know where I am. You know Mrs O'Connor's address. If ever you need me, I will come and fetch you."

Anna couldn't stop crying. Her heart was broken, and the people around her could make neither head nor tail of her sorrow. The weather was terrible. The clouds were pitch dark above her head and the rain bucketed down upon the deck of the boat. Thunder rolled, and lightning cracked above her head. It seemed like a biblical disaster as if the earth was destined to be destroyed. Anna shuddered. The dreadful storm was a bad omen. She began to dread going back to England. Elizabeth began to scream, and no matter how hard Anna tried to calm the child, she spent the entire journey unhappy. There was meagre shelter on deck. Anna had to stand under a flapping, collapsing awning. On this trip, Anna experienced the fury of the high seas, and she was terrified by its raw power. If Andrew was with her, she would have been safe. He would know what to do. He was her safe place. They would laugh through any situation. No matter how bad it was, he would explain what was happening and that everything would be alright. He would see the glory of nature, the weather, turbulent waves, and powerful currents, not the danger. Andrew could see the bright side and the miracle of everything. She missed him.

Liverpool had not changed. It was the same as always. A depressing array of soot-stained warehouses welcomed her. It would be the same in Manchester, probably worse. The torrential rain attached itself to the soot and coal dust in the atmosphere and rained down upon her, leaving her streaked in grey. Now she was as grey as the buildings around her.

She searched the waiting crowd. She was disappointed that Colin was not there to meet her. She had expected him to be there, and possibly give her a bunch of flowers. She waited for him until the wharf was empty. Eventually, she gave up. A young porter approached her, and she asked him to find her a cab that could take her to the station. Colin probably had an emergency to deal with. He was probably tending to something very important. Anna climbed aboard the train, and it steamed toward Manchester. Elizabeth continued to yowl. People stared at her, but there was nothing she could do. As the train puffed into the platform, there was nobody to welcome her at Piccadilly station either.

By the time she reached the front door to her Salford home, she and Elizabeth were exhausted. Anna went to the courtyard and opened the kitchen door. Her three friends, the household servants, were delighted to see her and grabbed Elizabeth from her as fast as they could. Anna went into the parlour and looked around. Something had changed, or rather, someone. She realised that it was her that had changed.

The atmosphere in the house felt dark and oppressive. She had no desire to be there. All the benefits of the convenient arrangement with Colin had gone. The only instinct she had was to run back to the station and escape. Yet, she couldn't do that. She had to meet her obligations to Colin Wheeler. She was his route to respectability with his public role as the successful, proud family man. Trapped and miserable, she was living in a prison with the door open.

Colin arrived well after midnight. He was drunk and loud. He greeted her with quick abrupt hello. It was not the warm personality that she was used to. She walked forward to greet him as affectionately as possible, but he stepped away from her, avoiding contact. Colin didn't waste much time in getting to the point.

"We have a few things that need settling," he slurred. I want you out of the house by tomorrow morning."

He hiccupped, then gave a loud boozy belch.

"Don't you want to see the baby?"

"No, it's not my child," he said meanly.

"What has happened?" she asked. "Why are you treating me this way?"

"You are bad for business, love. You are bad news. I should never have taken you in."

The romantic rejection was welcome, but the practicalities of it were not.

"I don't know where I can go," said Anna. "I don't have any money."

"Go and do what you're good at. You have slept with every man in Angel Meadows. That's what you're best at, and with luck, it'll bring in a few bob."

Anna was shocked she didn't know what had come over Colin. He had known everything about her when he married her and that she had only been with Mario.

"You can stay here under one condition," he grizzled, eyes rolling around as he spoke. "Providing no one has seen the child."

"No one has Colin, only the maids."

"Good. They don't matter. I'll silence them by threatening them with the sack."

He cupped her face with his rough hands and leaned in, the spittle landing on her skin as he spoke.

> "You must get rid of that illegitimate swine you have brought into this house. And then you will live here on my terms."

Anna tried to speak, but no words came out. Colin was sly. He knew that Anna would never give up the baby after three months together.

> "Get over to the workhouse in the morning and dump it there."
>
> "I can't!" She cried out. "I love her!"
>
> "You have pulled the wool over my eyes. That's what I will tell everyone," Colin mumbled to himself. "I will tell them that you are a fallen woman. That you lied to escape the Meadows and move out here. Everyone will understand why I am throwing you on the street, you dirty little shrew."

Raging, he struck her across the face.

> "You will not ruin my career," Colin lamented, almost in tears from a small mixture of self-pity and a lot of alcohol.

Anna was a meek person. She had never been a fighter and didn't know how to respond to the abuse.

> "I don't love you. I never loved you—I used you. And that wasn't worth it either. I am in love with somebody else!"

He accentuated the 'somebody' and was disappointed when Anna didn't immediately ask who.

"The sooner I get rid of you, the faster I can marry her."

Eventually, Anna gave him what he wanted.

"Who is she?"

Colin stared at her coldly.

"She is a woman who has a lot more to offer than you. That is all that I will tell you."

"You will tell me. Who is it? This fabulous new woman of yours? Consuelo Montagu, Duchess of Manchester?"

"Shady," Colin spat out.

Anna's jaw dropped. For once in her life, she spoke up for herself.

"How can marrying the town tart possibly be better than being married to me?"

"It's easy, sweetheart," he drawled, "she always knew who her father was. She hasn't mothered a baseborn child—and she's better in bed than you are!"

Humiliation and hurt surged through Anna's body. The happy days in Dublin were now just a fantasy. Real life was bitter and brutish. Colin had a point.

There were plenty of stains besmirching her reputation. What had she been thinking to hope that she had a future with a man like Andrew? Why would a man as wonderful as him consider a shameful woman like her? As soon as the truth was out, that would be the end of any chance with him.

Colin gulped down two glasses of whisky. He felt nothing for the young woman in front of him, but he was proud of his manly strength. He felt empowered and ready to perform his next ruthless act. Colin loved to use, destroy, and discard anyone he chose to. He was not finished with Anna—there was one more nail to drive into her coffin.

> "Get on the bed, sweetheart, and take your clothes off. You are still my wife."

Anna looked at him in horror. Surely, he didn't expect her to comply with his demands. Colin began to undress, then stood naked, flaccid, desperately trying to arouse himself sufficiently to abuse his wife one last time.

> "Come here, wench," he ordered, lurching towards her.

Fumbling those last drunken actions, Colin tripped over a thick rug. His knees buckled beneath him. He collapsed, then passed out. Anna ran to the nursery and lifted Elizabeth out of the little white cot. She couldn't leave her child to destiny like that.

The idea of a better life for her Elizabeth raced through her grey matter. More than ever, the Emerald Isle shone a beautiful, luscious green. But the industrialised world was a small place, and sooner or later, Colin would find her and expose her past, paint her in the worst possible light. He would ensure that the story would reach the newspaper, Andrew and his family's reputation would be ruined. All Mary's thoughts were jumbled and irrational. She was in no state of mind to be logical. She was filled with guilt, dread, and self-loathing. It was easy to crush Anna's soul. She had experienced rejection time and again.

The distraught mother looked down at little Elizabeth with tears streaming down her lovely face.

> "I am doing this for you, little one," she whispered into the baby's warm little ear.

It was almost daybreak. Anna tiptoed into Colin's study. She took a piece of paper from his drawer and began to write. Then she sealed the message in a plain white envelope and addressed it.

Whilst Elizabeth was dressed warmly and swaddled her in blankets, Anna didn't put on a coat or a hat. There was no time for that—she had to rectify her mistakes and flee the mean house.

She plodded towards Salford Bridge. Halfway across, she lay Elizabeth down on the cold ground and tucked the letter into the blanket. The child screamed blue murder. Anna blocked the noise from her mind. Onlookers reported that it was as if she was sleepwalking. The bridge was busy with people heading to work. They didn't take much notice of Anna. They were accustomed to seeing people behaving strangely. Being late for work was a more pressing concern.

Anna turned around and walked to the waist-high railing. She didn't bother to climb over it, simply leaning her torso over the steel bars, then heaving herself forward. Without much fuss, her top-heavy body flopped over the rail and plummeted into the icy, polluted water. Her leather boots filled with water making them as heavy as bricks. Her thick cotton clothes absorbed every ounce of liquid they could. She sank to the bottom of the river, the strong current dragging her downstream. Opening her eyes briefly, all she saw was a brown haze with detritus floating through it. Starved for air, instinctively, she gasped for breath. Her lungs filled with the diseased brown water, and she realised her mistake.

As dread and reality gave her a sucker punch, she wanted to turn around, but it was too late. Elizabeth was her world, her everything, and she wanted to tell Andrew Keegan that she loved him. Anna began to lose consciousness.

As her mind began to fade to black, she saw nothing. There were no lights to guide her. Her mother was not there with open arms to welcome her. There were no dead relatives waiting for her or divine angels of light to help her cross the abyss. She was alone. There was nothing, no one. Up on the bridge, everybody rushed to the railing and looked down to see if the girl had survived.

Only one woman ran toward the baby, ignorant of what was happening on the riverbank. She picked up Elizabeth and saw the corner of a crumpled envelope peeking out of the blankets.

Martha Havelock couldn't read, but she could recognise the shape of the layout. An address. Another passer-by snatched the note and saw there was an instruction to deliver the child to safety. A kind cabbie read the note, and the generous driver offered to take them to the centre of Manchester.

It took a while to reach their destination. As they neared the address, the houses and apartments became grand. This surprised her. She hoped that she would be lucky enough to receive a reward for her good deed. She would share it with the cab driver.

Tommy Thompson had watched the event from the muddy bank under the bridge, busy cleaning the hull of a barnacled-up old boat. When he heard the collective shouts of pedestrians on the bridge, he looked up to see what the fuss was about. All he saw was a woman in mid-air, then a splash. Tommy was in two minds whether to save her or not. He only had one set of clothes to his name. He debated the situation with himself for a few seconds then dived into the icy river. He hastened—her sodden body was sinking fast. Tommy was a skinny bag of bones. He had the opposite problem. He was struggling to dive deep enough to pull her out. On the third try, he took a deep breath and plunged below the surface. This time he saw a dull reflection of the dress and the face of an angel, hair surrounding it like a halo. He put out his hand and grabbed a hand full of hair. He pulled her toward him, but there was resistance. Tommy was close to giving up and letting go when he saw a rope descending toward him. One hand had Anna by the hair, the other tugged at the rope. The rope began to move, pulling them upward. Tommy broke the water and saw all the faces looking down at him. Two men on the bank began to pull Anna and her brave rescuer toward the shore. The whole event had taken a minute, but to those watching, it seemed like an age. Anna lay in the mud, and the men pounded her on her back.

Dark water exploded out of her mouth. Anna's lungs were on fire, and it felt as if the grit in the water had scoured her windpipe. She took in a deep breath. Although she was barely conscious, the sky above her was bright. She realised she was alive. God had granted her a second chance.

"It's Colin Wheeler's wife," someone cried from above.

"Send for him!" Tommy Thompson shouted back.

A young boy was dispatched to the club forthwith. Everyone knew who Colin Wheeler was and where to find him.

Within ten minutes, Colin arrived at the scene looking debonair but flustered. He acted like royalty and waved up at the crowd as he got out of the cab and made his way to the river bank, despite the annoyance that he had to dirty his shoes to reach his wife. She was a complete embarrassment. He had the whole of Salford watching him. How dare she try to take her own life?

Colin knew how to work a crowd and play to the gallery. He sacrificed his polished brogues and expensive suit and rushed into the muddy slush of the River Irwell. He had gone that far and decided that he may as well make the most of it. He reached Anna, fell to his knees, and pulled her to his chest, finally ruining his suit beyond repair. He calculated the value and swore under his breath.

Colin made a great show, even going as far as to wipe his tearful eyes.

> "Come on, my darling, let me take you home and care for you."

He kissed her forehead, clinging onto her until two of his supporters gently prised her from his grasp and moved her towards the road.

There were 'ohs' and 'ahs' from the bridge. He shed crocodile tears as he saw a lifeless Anna lugged onto a cart.

"Take her to my residence. I shall follow along and bring the doctor. You must pull through, darling! I can't live without you."

Keen to use the opportunity to his benefit, he stumbled to the bridge, muddied and filthy, the image of a humble hero battling against the odds.

"Well done, lad! I cannot thank you enough for your brave action!"

Tommy shrugged before Colin's arms enveloped him in a bear hug.

"Anyone would have done the same," said Tommy wriggling himself free.

"Fiddlesticks. You risked your life to try and save my wife's. You are a true hero."

Wheeler slapped Tommy on the back and shook his hand so hard the dazed and weary lad nearly wobbled over.

"What's your name, sonny?"

"Tommy, Sir."

"Well, Tommy, you shall be handsomely rewarded for your bravery."

The crowd roared as Colin milked the situation even more.

> "And thank you," he said, spinning on his heels, arms outstretched directly eyeballing all the onlookers, "for watching over her as she fell and shouting for help. I shall be eternally grateful to each and every one of you. Your loyal assistance will be etched on my heart forever!"

The clapping and cheering filled the black night sky.

As he played to the crowd, Wheeler said nothing about Elizabeth, and he was relieved no one mentioned her either. Hushing things up in Dublin meant the people of Manchester were yet to learn of Colin's fatherhood, and the full picture eluded them. He presumed the brat had fallen into the deathly river with her loathsome mother. Good. In the excitement of the rescue, no one had noticed the blanketed bundle being taken away by a ragged-looking woman.

Enthralled by the mighty orator, on that terrible night, no one picked up on his omission except for an ambitious young journalist, busy scribbling down every detail he overheard from the gossiping crowd.

11

DENIAL

Young Martha Havelock climbed two flights of stairs to reach the residence of Mrs Mary Riddle, her head spinning round, eyeing every unfamiliar detail. Finally, reaching the top of a highly polished mahogany landing, there was only one enormous door before her. That was it. She looked down at the little bundle in her arms. Swallowing hard, Martha grabbed the cool brass doorknocker and banged loudly.

Footsteps clickety-clacked along the tiled hallway, and a key turned in the lock before the heavy black door swung open. The woman didn't greet Martha. She stood in the doorway and beady eyes looking her up and down, nose twitching, smelling the stench of Salford emanating from the strange woman. The accompanying baby both irritated and worried her.

Martha would never forget the cold woman's face for as long as she lived.

"Yes?" growled Mary. "What do you want?"

"I have a letter for you."

As Martha reached out to give Mary the letter, it was snatched from her hand in mid-air. Ripped open with such haste, the letter tore a little along with the envelope.

Dear Mary

I can't put my Elizabeth through a life of torment.

I can only give her a better life by sacrificing my own.

You are the only person I know who can help her.

I am ashamed of myself. I can't continue knowing that my choices will tarnish Elizabeth's life forever.

Please look after your niece so that I may die in peace.

Your loving sister,

Anna

Mary read the letter twice. She looked at the baby in Martha's arms but didn't go near it, feeling no compassion for the child, whatever its name was. She didn't ask Martha how she came upon Elizabeth, nor did she care.

Mary made her decision in a split second.

"I don't know the person in this letter." snapped Mary.

"But Ma'am, it is addressed to you!"

Mary stared at the woman with menace.

"That child is not my family."

"Why would this letter be in the blanket, then?" Martha blurted out.

"Get away from my door and take that child with you. If you bother me again, I will have you arrested."

Martha was terrified. This wealthy woman could cause a lot of trouble for her if she reported her to the coppers. The door slammed loudly in the visitor's face. Inside, Mary still had the letter in her hand. She decided she would do well to get rid of it.

'So typical of Anna.'

Mary didn't need to revisit her decision. She would not raise her sister's child, let alone her own. She wanted nothing to do with the child and never wanted to hear or see it again.

"Who was at the door?" asked Alec.

"A woman wanting me to take in Anna's base child."

Alec frowned.

"I don't understand."

"Anna has taken her life."

Alec's eyes widened at the callously delivered news.

"But why did you send the child away? It is your family! What will happen to the poor mite?"

"Have you forgotten about my trip to Liverpool so soon? Risking my life to be rid of an unwanted child. How dare my sister request that I will look after hers?"

Alec was hurt to the core and didn't, couldn't, argue. He chose to ignore the words. Nothing that he said would change Mary's cold heart. Besides, there were contractual terms to consider. Alec was beginning to have misgivings about having married the shrew, a mean woman who lacked empathy, never performing a good deed or showing a shred of kindness. Neither man nor beast received any mercy.

His jaw clenched. He had made a mistake. Living with this creature of darkness was different to meeting with her occasionally. She was a lunatic. Their intimate life had taken a turn for the worse as well. Mary had slowly introduced violence and abuse into their physical relationship. This didn't sit well with Alec. After Mary's abortion, he had left his marriage bed and moved to another bedroom. Now, with her main benefit diminished, he knew that it would not be long before he left her for good.

Mary was as hard-nosed as ever. Alec Riddle watched Mary crumple up the note and toss it into the fire, and smirk as it disappeared.

> "We will never discuss this again, Alec. Do you understand?"

Riddle leaned back in his chair and looked at her over his glasses, his eyelids narrowing. He felt the cold dislike that had been brewing for months finally take hold. Disgust rose up like bile, and in that moment, he no longer loved her.

His reply surprised her, but it didn't move her to remorse.

> "Get out of my study, and don't come into this room ever again."

Poor Martha Havelock had no choice but to trudge all the way to the Prestwich Workhouse. Exhausted from the walk and carrying the baby, she pounded on the great wooden door until someone opened it.

> "What's the name?" asked the mistress.
>
> "Martha, Martha Havelock."
>
> "We are so full. I don't know where I will put you and the child."
>
> "Just the child, Ma'am. I found her on Salford Bridge."
>
> "What is her mother's name?"

"I don't know. Her mother jumped over the railings and left her on the pavement."

"Really?" said the mistress, having heard plenty of those stories. "And it's definitely not yours?"

"No, ma'am. I swear!"

"What is its name?"

"There was a note that said Elizabeth."

"Where is the note now?"

Martha told the mistress about her visit to Mary.

"The woman said she didn't know the child and refused to take her." pleaded Martha. "She was such a mean woman. I am quite sure that she was telling the truth. But I can't understand how a woman could be that vile to someone in her family. Looked like she had a bob or two from the address."

"Well, we have too many babies here called Elizabeth," said the matron, "We will call her Ellie."

Martha smiled and nodded. The matron wrote the name in her book.

"Surname?"

"I don't know," Martha said.

"Right then, it will be Prestwich. We will send somebody to find out who the young mother is."

Martha handed the baby over to the woman, who smiled down at the child.

"Hello, Ellie Prestwich. Welcome to your new home."

As she proudly trudged back to Salford, Martha had a good feeling about the kindly woman. Elizabeth—Ellie—was in good hands.

The tot would not be with the workhouse mistress for long. In winter, Prestwich workhouse was full to bursting, and she had no space for Elizabeth—even if she was tiny.

In the morning, she was forced to send the child to the local orphanage. It was a miserable hole, and the people who ran it numbered as many as the children who occupied it. Elizabeth was allocated a beleaguered wet nurse, drained from tending four other children at the same time.

It was no surprise that there were regular outbreaks of disease amongst children and that an average of fourteen babies died per month. The small creatures suffered in impoverished, unhygienic conditions. There was also the cold to contend with. The carers would reach the babies in the morning only to find ice-cold stiff little bodies. Only the lucky and the strongest survived.

The staff at the facility had long since lost the passion and drive to care for others. They were given the responsibility of looking after people, while living in abject poverty themselves. The orphanage rules were cruel and mostly unnecessary, but they were implemented as a desperate measure to make the administrators' lives easier.

The gaunt widow, Mrs Howick, was given the responsibility of nursing Elizabeth. She did her job resentfully. Only there because she needed a job to survive, she had been doing it for the last five years, since the death of her last baby. She felt as if her body was constantly being devoured by small parasites, who were no better than ticks. Her resentment was exhibited in the rough manner that she treated the infants.

Elizabeth was lucky her wet nurse was in the orphanage. The role, better paid than labouring, attracted greedy women just as much as the caring ones. Outside of institutions, infant deaths were not always due to a lack of care or nutrition. Money played a part. A lucrative income stream could come to a callous woman enrolling her own or the nursed children in multiple burial societies profiting from multiple deaths caused by illness and a lack of nutrition.

Like many women, Howick took the position because she would have been destitute without it. Working around the clock, the only advantage was that she was given basic lodgings and was fed very well.

The moment Ellie Prestwich was handed to Mrs Howick, the hard woman looked down at her and sensed something amiss about the child. Mrs Howick couldn't identify precisely what it was, but the infant irritated her. Maybe it was the constant fidgeting and the propensity to chortle loudly for hours on end, waking the other children in her care. Even at this tender age, Elizabeth had the heart of a lion and a determination to survive.

The gummy tot smiled joyously. To a world-weary woman like Howick, she was annoying cheerful. No matter how many babies were screaming at the top of their lungs, little Elizabeth laughed. It would have been easy for her to become a favourite, but Howick had no capacity to love. According to her, it would have been easier to just drown this unwanted child in the river, like folks did with a brick and sack full of kittens.

The orphanage was bleak and draughty, and nobody tried to make it more comfortable. Only the most basic standards of accommodation and care were provided. There were simply no funds available for even the most humble of treats.

Now a few months old, Mrs Howick decided Elizabeth should be fed a mixture of milk and watery gruel. It seemed to keep her and the other babies satisfied for the moment. At this tender age, the babies were controllable, but the problems started when they began to walk. Eventually, the nurses would tie them down in their cots or beds, and they would be left to scream for hours while incompetent house mothers ignored them. Amidst all this chaotic activity, Ellie Prestwich remained a cheerful little soul.

Mrs Howick noted Elizabeth's complexion. It was so different to the other orphans. Elizabeth had a mop of black curls, dark eyes to match and a beautiful olive shade. The child stuck out like a sore thumb amongst the other little rosy-cheeked, ivory-skinned orphans. Even so young, it was evident that Elizabeth was going to be beautiful.

Irked by the swarthy-looking child, Mrs Howick suspected that Elizabeth may be of gipsy stock. Like most other folks, she hated gipsies. It was hard to empathise with a gipsy harlot who hurled herself off a bridge, leaving the child alone. Now the hateful thing was challenging her.

In her exhausted mind, Mrs Howick built the case until she had convinced herself that it was true. That afternoon, she shared her thoughts with another nurse. From that moment on, the information was conveyed as truth.

She was instantly an outcast, but Elizabeth didn't know that.

12

HEADLINE NEWS

Mario Perreira was shocked and consumed with guilt when he read the news that Anna had attempted to take her life. A week later, the news reached Dublin. Andrew Keegan read the headlines as he sat in one of his and Anna's favourite tea rooms. He shoved his hand in this pocket and hurriedly threw money onto the table, and escaped hastily. He walked around the corner, put his head against a red brick wall and sobbed.

Both men noted that there was no mention of Anna's child, Elizabeth. They assumed that the baby would be in the care of Colin Wheeler.

The news about Anna was emblazoned across the front page of every newspaper. Mario Perreira was driven to anger that he had never experienced before. This time the fury was not directed at Colin Wheeler. Mario would go and see him later. His fury was directed toward his mother. The old woman was an unyielding bully. Anna's pain was a stain on her character, not his, but no doubt he would still cop the flack for it. Over the years, Mama Perriera had dictated how other people run their lives. Like a vice clamping tighter and tighter, she had crushed his father's spirit. Mario was sick of her constant criticism. Her endless critique pivoted on her religious beliefs, which never reflected any good Christian values, only selfishness.

Mario Perreira knew that if he had been strong enough to stand up to his mother, he could have saved suicidal Anna the desolation she must have felt. He had neglected her, driven her into another man's arms, then discarded her when she was desperate and pregnant with his child. When she announced that she was expecting, he had been horrified. Having his roving days come to an end held no appeal. At least being forced to marry a subservient wife held more promise for extramarital affairs than if he married delicate Anna, who might expect him to be faithful.

It took some months for him to realise that his wife Conchita was a bore who couldn't perform her marital duties passionately because certain acts were taboo. Lovemaking was only for marriage and procreation, and this idea was firmly indoctrinated into her repressed mind. She pushed him away as much as possible, unaware that was into the arms of other women.

On the infrequent occasions, the married couple made love, Conchita ensured that she went to confession and put extra money into the poor box. Only in retrospect did Mario realise the gem he had in the sensual beauty that was Anna. Yes, he had been furious when he learned that she was pregnant, but at the same time, he had accepted that the child was his.

In this hour of maturation, he often wondered how it would have been if he had married Anna. His life would have been filled with laughter, and there would have been fire in his nights. The frigid woman he was married to suddenly held no appeal. The idea of his mother expecting him to pump out one child after another to populate the earth with good Christians seemed undignified—and desperately dull.

He was reaching the stage where he would have given anything for a simple life with a woman who completed him, not kept just his yapping mother at bay.

He slumped and put his head in his hands. It was too late. His mother had already insisted his life run a particular course. Her course. And he had foolishly followed it. Mama Perreira only cared if he fathered umpteen children, which was all that marriage was about for her.

Many of Mario's evenings spent away from home were a feeble, lustful attempt at contraception. Mama Perreira was beginning to suspect that Conchita was barren. A few weeks ago, she interrogated her daughter-in-law on the subject, who confessed her son was not performing his marital obligations. The fuming mother had chastised Mario about his woeful, lustful behaviour, but he didn't care anymore. He couldn't face a future centred on fulfilling the archaic principles of breeding.

Mario flung the kitchen door open. His mother, father and wife were sitting at the table. On the surface, it was a regular Sunday morning, and the family was fulfilling an old tradition of drinking coffee and eating pastries before cooking the afternoon meal. Later, the kitchen would be invaded by aunts, sisters and cousins who would prepare enough food to feed a small European nation.

Mario took the newspaper and slammed it down on the table in front of his mother. Mama Perreira jumped in her seat, and his father turned around, flabbergasted by his bad manners. A timid Conchita sat silently on the other side of the table, not bold enough to question him.

Mario couldn't restrain himself.

> "Look what you have done, Mama, look what you have done!" Mario blurted out. "And you are not excused blame, Papa. This is all because you couldn't take charge of your wife!"

Papa Perreira glanced down at the newspaper, and his mouth dropped open.

> "She tried to take her life?" he stammered, the question stupid considering the lurid headline's details.

> "Can't you read Papa? Of course, she did. She threw herself off Salford Bridge because she was miserable and had to raise an illegitimate child. Yes, Papa, she committed the ultimate sin of taking her life because an orphan has more legitimacy than a child spawned out of wedlock."

Mama Perreira began screaming at the top of her voice as she always did when she insisted upon her own way.

> "I told you that girl was no good, Mario. I told you she would come back to haunt you. I told you that she would cause trouble. You were told to keep away from her a long time ago—with good reason."

Suddenly, the three of them realised that Conchita was in the room. Tearful, she sat in awe, watching the row between the three of them escalate, trying to make sense of the jumble of facts bombarding her. Until now, the secret of Mario impregnating Anna had been hidden by the tight-lipped Perriera trio from everyone, including poor Conchita. Confused, her watery eyes scanned the headline repeatedly, each time the truth hitting a little harder as the sordid picture became clearer.

Eventually, the puzzle pieces started to lock into place, and she was brave enough to speak.

> "Mario, what is it? What has gone wrong? Who is this girl? This child?" she mouthed.

Enraged, the others didn't notice Conchita's quiet mutterings.

> "What is this Anna to you now? It's in the past. She has a husband. Or rather, had one," Mama Perreira yelled.

> "Are you really that stupid? She bore me a child," boomed Mario so loud the room seemed to shake. "A child I have a responsibility to—wherever the poor mite is! I must look for her."

Conchita crumpled from the agonising pain of his confession.

> "Get out, Mario. Get out. We will not discuss this in front of Conchita."

Mama Perriera took Mario by the arm and tried to nudge him toward the door, desperate to get them out of earshot of a disconsolate Conchita. Mario was having none of it. He wrenched his elbow free. In that instant, he became a real man, no longer a timid son controlled by his matriarchal mother. Now, he was beyond taking orders from either of his parents.

"Tell me where my child is! You tell me what happened to this baby. All this article says is the troubled mother arrived with a child, and then its whereabouts became unclear as the crisis unfolded."

"The child is not your problem anymore," said Mama Perreira. "That child was a problem since it was conceived. Don't you dare go to Colin's home looking for it. I told you that running around with that harpy was going to cost you everything. And if anyone sees you visiting Wheeler, his henchmen will burn down your father's business!"

"I am responsible for that child, Mama."

Conchita's eavesdropping head slid down against the door frame, her spirit crushed, dreams shattered.

"What is this about another child Mario? You have never said anything to me about a child," she sobbed.

"Mario, if you say anything, it could mean the end of your marriage to Conchita. Under these circumstances, she can have your marriage annulled. Do you want that? You shut up right now," ordered Mama Perreira.

"I am not going to spend my life watching Colin Wheeler raise my child."

By this time, the young, naïve, and innocent Conchita was bereft. She never expected anything bad from her husband. Even on the nights when he never came home, she always put it down to him working hard for his family.

> "I never wanted Conchita anyway. She was never my choice, forced upon me by you and my aunts—and now you expect me to be happy?" Mario snarled.
>
> "Do you think you would have been happy with that hussy? You are fooling yourself," yelled the old woman.
>
> "She was no hussy, Mama," Mario roared with tears in his eyes, "she was a virgin when I met her."
>
> "Get out, Mario. Don't come back until you've come to your senses!"

Mario lurched at her throat with his outstretched hands. His mother reached for a knife on the work-top. Papa Perreira looked knew that he if didn't separate them, one would murder the other.

As the old man bravely intervened, Conchita had seen and heard enough. She rushed from the room and went to the bedroom. She collapsed in a heap of tears. The truth had been told. Mario had got another girl pregnant. A girl who was now dead. Her marriage was a sham, arranged by her controlling mother-in-law, not the fairytale meeting of two soul mates she had imagined. Her resentful husband was a hateful lothario who thought nothing of lying to her and breaking her heart.

Putting on her coat and bonnet, the house was in such disarray that nobody noticed the tearful woman slip out of the house with the twins, planning to return to her father's home and never see her awful husband again.

In the tussle of fists and elbows, Papa Perreira looked at his wife. He had never seen her so hard and venomous.

> "I never want to see you again," she screamed into Mario's face. "You are not my son."

Eventually, the old man pushed the breathless pair apart.

> "Now, now, Mama," said Papa Perreira gently. "Mario is going nowhere. Sending him away is not going to solve the problem. Who is going to look after Conchita?"
>
> "That's not my concern. I want him out of the business. There are enough people here to see to Conchita," she shouted at the top of her voice.
>
> "No, Esmerelda."

The henpecked husband had not called his wife by her name in years, and she spun around and looked at him.

"No more. I have had enough of you!"

Papa Perreira banged his hand on the table so loudly that the brawling pair jumped.

"I am not going to throw my son away because you are worried about what other people think. It's been over a year, and still, no one knows about the child."

Mama Perreira pointed her finger at him.

"How dare you to speak to me like this? Telling me how this family should be run!"

Papa Perreira looked at her and spoke fiercely.

"This is my house. I've worked to look after you. You are my wife. This time you have gone too far. You are going to do what I tell you to from now on. I am not putting my son out of this house. I used to love you with my heart and soul, but now you have become a horrible old woman. We wouldn't be in this situation if it was not for your mean ways and evil tongue. Get out of this room. I don't want to see you for the rest of the day."

"But the family is coming. It is Sunday. Do not tell me—"

He didn't allow her to finish the sentence.

> "—Be damned the family, Esmerelda! Get out of my sight."

It was the first time that Mario had ever heard his father curse. Mama Perreira looked at her husband. It was the first time in twenty-five years that he spoke to her this way. She knew that she pushed her husband too far, and there was no telling how he might respond. To avoid his wrath, Mrs Perreira did as she was told. She shut up and didn't say another word. She haughtily left the room and retired to her bedroom, but the time she reached it, her arrogance had dissipated, and she burst into tears.

Esmerelda Perreira was a very worried woman.

13

NEVER TO RETURN

Bernard Errington strode down Angel Street, a towering, confident man in a snow-white uniform pressed to perfection. He wore a long navy-blue coat that reached mid-calf. Mavis McCrae noted that the epaulettes on his shoulders had changed. He had received a promotion.

The mariner reached the door of his wife's home. He never considered it his own and knocked on the door boldly. The door was opened by a young woman with a child on her hip.

"Yes, Mister?"

"Where are the people who live here? My wife and children live here," Bernard demanded.

The young woman looked bewildered. Afraid of the man and intimidated by his official status, she was relieved to see Mavis running across the street to her rescue.

"Hello, Bernard." called Mavis, "How are you, love."

Bernard had a premonition that Mavis had bad news.

"Mavis," he said with a nod.

"Come over and have some tea."

"I am in no mood for tea, Mavis," Bernard said abruptly, at once regretting it.

To stand a better chance of getting what he wanted, he changed to a polite tone.

"Do you know where Jeanie is?".

"I am sorry, Bernard," muttered Mavis, "I only have bad news."

Bernard's blood ran cold.

"Poor old Jeanie, well—she died a while ago."

"How? Why?"

Mavis didn't know how she could lessen the blow for this dignified and loyal family man.

"Consumption, she didn't suffer. It was fast," Mavis lied.

"Was Dicky there at the end?"

"No," said Mavis. "He was murdered a few months before by the Scuttlers."

Bernard was in a living nightmare.

"Mary?"

"Nobody knows where Mary is. Elsie says word has it she may have left for London, but we aren't sure."

"Anna?"

Mavis shuffled about, thinking of the best way to out things.

"Come on, woman! Tell me!"

"She jumped off Salford Bridge just recently. Troubled she was. Tried to end her life. They carted her off to her husband's house. Everyone says she was dead when they pulled her out. Some folks say she left her little baby on the bridge. Others said she jumped in with it. Truth be told, no one knows what happened."

"Someone must know something?"

Mavis pursed her lips to one side and shook her head slowly.

"Who did she marry? Where was her husband during this mess? Surely he knows what happened to his child?"

Mavis told the story of Anna's marriage to Colin Wheeler. She apologised for only knowing vague details, snippets of information that had relayed along the rows and embellished as they went along. As Bernard absorbed the news that his beloved little family was no more, he felt his legs weaken. He crumpled down the sooty brick wall, falling to the ground like an old newspaper. The pristine hems of his trousers soaked up the mud caking the cobbles as he began to weep quietly.

"Come, come, my love," said Mavis gently.
"Let's go and have that cuppa, should we."

A dishevelled-looking Bernard Errington stood up shakily, his uniform caked in dirt. In no position to argue, he let Mavis help him across the street to partake in her hospitality.

"What are you going to do now? Are you going to find Mary? Look for the baby?"

"I only have two days in Manchester. I have no time to find them. Besides, where would I start? I'll see if I can take some extra leave and try to find them. It's all so confusing. Everything I hold dear to me is gone."

"Will you write to me, Bernard? Let me know how you're getting on? If I hear anything, I'll pass the information on."

"Of course, Mavis," he agreed, though he never wrote and nor spoke to Mavis again.

For the second time in his life, Bernard sought the refuge of the sea.

In Ireland, the week proved to be a struggle for Andrew Keegan. He couldn't accept that Anna had been driven to take her life. What could have been so dreadful that she had wanted to die? The Anna that he knew would never have left her child behind to an uncertain future. He regretted that he had not convinced her to stay in Ireland. He should have tried harder to keep her in Dublin. He would have given her a good life. His family had the power to protect her from Colin Wheeler should he have come chasing after his young wife. Besides, why would he look for her? A rumour had circulated from a sailor down at the docks that Colin Wheeler had been in an affair with a brothel owner. This may have explained why Anna had never received letters from her husband during her residency in Ireland.

Andrew Keegan climbed the steps to Mrs O'Connor's front door. He knocked slowly and without energy. She opened the door to a very sad young man who she hardly recognised for sorrow. Putting her arms around him, he seemed to slump on her shoulder.

> "Come now, come now," she patted his back as he cried softly. "Come now, lad. Let's have some tea. We can have a talk."
>
> "What could have happened that she killed herself? Why would she leave Elizabeth? She would never have discarded her child."

"Oh, my sweetheart, I can't tell you what has happened. All I know is that I agree with you this is a terrible time for us."

"I've never said this to anyone Mrs O'Connor, but I was in love with Anna. If she had six babies from six other men, I would have loved them all," Andrew said with a sad smile.

"I loved Elizabeth. I never wanted them to go back to Manchester. Can we trust her husband to look after the bairn?"

"Aww, lad, there are so many questions and no answers."

"I don't know where to lay the blame. I want someone to answer for this. Her family? Her husband? The feckless father?"

Mrs O'Connor nodded and sipped her tea.

"I must go and find that child. I must find her. I was the first person to hold her when she entered this world. I am going to see Colin Wheeler. I need to talk to him."

"But do you think that is wise?" asked Mrs O'Connor. "He is a very powerful man."

"Where else could Elizabeth be? I can't see her being anywhere else. I presume she is named and registered as Elizabeth Wheeler. I am sure that he would not allow a child with his name to disappear. If she did survive, there would be a scandal if he was seen to discard his own flesh and blood."

"I don't know what to tell you, Andrew. I've got a feeling that you're going to do what do you feel is best. Just be careful of Colin Wheeler. He is a very powerful man."

"I never flaunt my status, Mrs O'Connor," said Andrew Keegan softly, "but my family is also powerful, and I will use it to my advantage should I need to."

14

DRASTIC ACTIONS

Once more, the aftermath of Anna's jump had shamed her husband, and he was furious that she had brought such negative attention upon him at this pivotal stage of his political career. He had done everything possible to turn the negative publicity into a positive. He had managed to emerge a hero, earning the public's admiration, especially when he put on the tearful show and crushed her to his chest in sorrow. But there would be awkward questions. After all, wives of successful men do not throw themselves into the Irwell.

The cart dropped Anna at the house in Salford, and the three maids rushed out to greet her. Anna lay on the car motionless, covered in mud from top to toe. One of the women saw a foot and peeled back a dirty grey tarpaulin. Underneath, Anna looked so frail. No one could see if she was breathing.

"She jumped off the Salford bridge," said the driver. "Tried to take her life. Luckily, Tommy Thompson was there. He jumped into the river and fished her out. Quite a thing it was. People gawping over the edge wondering if she'd pull through."

Late and keen to get home, the callous driver didn't care whether the woman was still alive or not. He skipped off the seat and prepared to lug the body off the flatbed of the wagon.

The three women looked at each other. They couldn't believe what they were hearing. Vibrant, happy Anna must have been very miserable to throw herself into the filthy Irwell River. They were aware of Colin's affair with Shady, and they had heard the rumpus in the bedroom the night that Anna returned home from Dublin. However, they had not heard Colin instructing his wife to get rid of the baby. Where was she?

"We'll take her in, thank you," snapped Julia, the housekeeper. "Where is her child?"

"There's no sign of a nipper, just her. Hurry up and sort this. I want to get off. Should have finished my shift an hour ago," the driver tutted.

The three of them lifted Anna gently off the cart, carried her into the house, and laid her corpse on the kitchen table.

"S'pose we'd better make plans to speak to the local undertaker," said Cook, the words choking her.

At the same time, Colin Wheeler arrived and crashed through the back door in a fury, honking of booze, childless.

"What the hell do you think that you are doing, woman?" shouted Colin.

The servants were baffled? Why shout at a body? The rumpus caused Anna to stir. As her core temperature rose fractionally higher, her eyes flickered, and her shallow breathing became deeper and laboured.

Putting her fingers on her carotid artery and her ear to the poor waif's mouth, Sally whispered:

"She's alive!"

The women sighed with relief. Colin Wheeler trembled with anger, using all his might not to smother the girl there and then. That would have to wait.

"We need to get her sorted, Sir," replied Julia.

"Yes, yes!" Colin agreed begrudgingly.

"Fetch the doctor, Sir."

Colin obstinately folded his arms and stood rooted to the spot. Panicking, the older women took charge.

"Let's get her warm then, ladies," said Cook. "That river water she swallowed is so filthy, it will be surprising if she survives."

Colin smirked.

"Right poisonous it is. Surely get her cholera, it will," Sally added.

His drunken smirk widened further as he thought of her sudden demise. Soon, he would be free of his tedious embarrassment of a wife and finally in the loving embrace of Shady. As his thoughts turned back to himself, his expression blackened once more. The scandal would also make him the talk of the town, and not in the way he would have liked. Although Wheeler had heroically pulled her from the mud, there would be an army of fingers pointing at him, wondering why she would be driven to such a terrible crime. Was it something to do with him?

"What a bloody fool she is," Colin hissed. "What did she think she was doing? Her constant recklessness will be the ruin of my career, ungrateful little witch. I should have left her in the gutter where I found her."

The three women looked at him, shocked by his words, but he was too annoyed to even notice their disgust. They decided they would fight for Anna's survival even if he wouldn't. With one grabbing both legs, the other two took an arm each, and they began to slide her off the table.

"Stop right there!" Colin reprimanded. "You will not traipse through my house with her in that condition. Get her cleaned up here. She's not lying in one of my beds in that state, caked in mud. It's bad enough that I've had to dirty my shoes and suit! And look at my oak table! Someone had better sort clean that if you know what's good for you!"

The women lowered her onto the kitchen flagstones. Unsupported, her lolling head banged onto the floor, bringing a look of pleasure to Colin's hard face.

"Can't you be careful for once, Sally !" Cook moaned.

Julia kneeled next to Anna, stroking the poor woman's hair, all clammy, filthy, and knotted.

"Go and get a pail of hot water, Cook. And bring me as many rags as you can find. Master, get one of the horse's rugs for her to lay on while we clean her."

Colin was rooted to the spot. Julia was left to run to the stable.

"She's turning blue, Julia!" shrieked Sally.

"It's all that wet hair and clothing. It's giving her a chill. Losing too much heat, she is. The blankets are doing nothing."

"What should we do about it?" asked Julia hesitantly.

"There isn't time to dry it. Cut it all off," said Cook, "I know that it's a terrible thing to do, but we have no choice. Scissors, Sally !"

The shaken chambermaid did as she was told. Cook returned with the bucket of hot water and a cake of carbolic soap. Julia began to hack Anna's clothes off. As layers of fabric peeled back, they saw more of Anna's blue skin. The little bit of warmth that she clung to was gone, and she began to shiver and shake. Cook plunged a thick towel in the hot water, folded it, and put it on the woman's exposed neckline. Seconds later, it had cooled against her cold flesh.

"We need to submerge her. This pail is not enough."

"I told you you're not taking her through my house like that," ordered Colin. "Do the best that you can with what you've got."

The cook looked at him in disgust. She was about to pick up a hefty pudding basin and smash it over his head to teach him a lesson once and for all. The disgusting man deserved to be beaten. But she stopped short of picking it up. If she was thrown out of the house, Anna would suffer more at the hands of Colin. They were all glad when he stomped off to get himself a stiff drink.

Cook fetched her coat and put it over Anna. Carefully one limb was exposed at a time and thoroughly scrubbed. The hot water hardly helped, cooling as quickly it was sponged on. Her body was in shock, and by the time they reached her hair with the scissors, she had lost consciousness.

Colin ominously reappeared, a glass of Scotch in his hand, surveying their every move as he planned his next. He did nothing to help.

As he loomed large over Julia, her hot tears dripping down as she cut off Anna's hair, one lock at a time. The knotted muddy mess lay on the floor beside her. The sight delighted Colin.

"That will do," he barked after an hour.

"Carry her to the guest bedroom."

Cook reached for her coat to protect the young woman's modesty. It slid off one side and onto the floor. She lurched to recover it.

"No! Carry her as she is," snapped Colin.

He watched as they struggled to ascend the stairs carrying Anna's naked body between them, legs akimbo, her unconscious head bouncing over multiple stairs. Something about the unfolding image of his wife's vulnerable position filled him with a perverse pleasure, and he considered taking advantage of Anna when she lay alone in the bedroom one last time before he smothered her with a pretty, frill-trimmed pillow. He tipped his head back and through the last of the Scotch down his gullet, then wiped the dribble off his chin with the back of his hand.

Going off to pour another drink, Wheeler was already making detailed plans on how he would ravish his unconscious wife while his mistress slept snugly in his bed. It was going to be delicious.

Sally heaped a wobbly stack of coals and firelighters in the grate and lit them. Not caring about the dizziness, she blew and blew to get the orange flames to lick upwards and take a firm hold of the ebony coal.

Julia and Cook dragged the rug out of the way and pulled the heavy iron bed as close to the fire as was safe.

"When she comes round, let's try to get some hot tea into her," Sally cooed.

The other two gave a sly sideways glance, not feeling the same sense of optimism for Anna's future.

"Can you please get us some tea or broth?" Julia asked Cook. "And bring a dessert spoon. We'll probably have to feed it to her, poor thing."

Cook was grateful to get out of the oppressive room. She couldn't bear the idea of watching young Anna die.

Slowly but surely, Anna began to warm up, but it took a few hours before she regained consciousness.

Her voice was gruff, scoured by the filth that she had swallowed. Her throat was a swollen, hot mess. Her lungs burned as they fought against the damage they had incurred in the Irwell. Sally excused herself and went looking for Colin. She found him sitting in the library, puffing on a Cuban cigar.

> "Sir, we need a doctor. She needs help. Please, can we send for a doctor?"
>
> "I am not paying for a doctor," Colin stated coldly. "I am not spending another penny on that woman or a moment of that time. She is an embarrassment and has brought her problems on herself, not me. Any more of your silly requests, and it'll be the work-house for you. I'll make sure you never work in this city again."

Sally, young, inexperienced, and terrified of her boss, backed out of the room, stumbling awkwardly as she went. Colin took great pleasure in her fear.

If—when—Anna died, it would save Colin Wheeler a lot of trouble. There would be no need to make excuses for her shameful behaviour or take responsibility for the tiresome sadness that would overcome her as their sham of a marriage rumbled on. Changing his mind, rather than hastening her death by his own hand, he would make it as difficult as possible for the staff to help her, and if the gods were on his side, she would be dead within two days. Nobody would lay ever the blame at his feet. All his staff would keep quiet if they knew what was good for them.

Within the hour, Anna opened her eyes. Julia and Cook stopped their investigation as to Elizabeth's likely whereabouts. Both were praying the wee girl wasn't tangled up the junk thrown into the bottom of the river. The shock of discovering her cherished baby was missing might have finally finished the poor mother off. If Anna became panicked and breathless, who knows how it might end.

Unable to move her body, Anna was overcome with exhaustion. Every joint and muscle ached. They had tried to sit her up, but it had not gone well. They had wondered if lying flat was better if there was more water to come from her lungs. Her throat burnt like fire, and she could only move her eyes. She saw Julia above her and Sally's shadow next to her, stoking the fire. For a few minutes, she was disoriented, but when she realised where she was, she panicked. She couldn't see or hear Elizabeth. She tried to cry out, but her throat was on fire every time she tried to move her tongue or swallow.

"Baby," she rasped.

Julia could hardly hear her, even when she bent in close.

"Baby!" she rasped again.

Julia had to think quickly. She didn't want Anna to panic, so she answered nonchalantly as she ran her fingers through the poor woman's stubbly hair.

> "Relax, my angel, everything will be fine. Elizabeth is well looked after."

Sally kicked Julia in the shin, but she ignored it.

Cook took the small pot from beside the fire and made some lukewarm tea with sugar and milk. They tried offering the cup to her lips, but it was pointless. Even though the tea was tepid, Anna could hardly swallow it.

> "Come now, sweetheart," said Cook, reaching for the spoon. "You have to take this in, so you do. Come on, lass. Do it for Elizabeth if not yourself."

Anna did the best she could. Half an hour later, finishing the first meagre cupful, she was relieved it made her feel a bit stronger in spirit. Alas, the pain still tore through her lungs as though they had been scorched. It took two days before Anna could sit up properly. Colin slowed her recovery with a well-placed hurtful comment.

> "As far as I am concerned, the child is dead. It looked dark, like Perriera—nothing like me at all. The sooner you tell everyone that it has exited this world, the better. Think of something."

Anna had a vague recollection of writing the note and pushing it into the folds of the swaddling blankets, but she wasn't one hundred per cent sure. Maybe he knew something? Maybe her child was dead? Colin hoped the lie would demoralise Anna enough to give up hope and sink into a deep despair that would finally finish her off.

Keen to maintain his rod-of-iron control, he summoned the staff to his study and gave them a stark warning.

> "If any of you dare divulge anything that happens under this roof, you will suffer nothing short of death at the hands of my henchmen. Is that clear?"

The fearful women nodded.

> "And any mention of that blasted baby, within these walls or without, will result in a severe beating. It died in the river. That's all you need to know."

Colin was so busy threatening his staff that he had not heard the front door open. Always loud and obnoxious, Shady stood in the hallway listening to him. Although she was his mistress, she was not a cruel woman. On the contrary, she had helped many young women out of trouble, and she was a rare procuress who genuinely cared about the girls who worked for her. It was how she guaranteed their loyalty. Her empathy had built a powerful, profitable business.

Every girl knew the cruel treatment they could experience elsewhere and were never tempted to stray.

Julia came out of the study on the brink of tears and walked straight into Shady, unaware that the woman had been standing there for some time listening to Colin's ranting. Shady grabbed Julia by the shoulder and roughly pulled her ear towards her, and murmured:

> "When I finish with Mr Wheeler, I want to speak to you. Understand?"

It had been one of the most dreadful days of Julia's life, and now she was afraid it would become worse. She didn't know what the woman wanted from her, but she nodded her head and exited as fast as she could.

Julia scurried off to the kitchen. Later, she told Sally and Cook what Shady had said. She didn't have the faintest clue what the woman wanted to tell her. Hopefully, she just needed new linen on their bed. The housekeeper tried to put the request in the back of her mind and went back to Anna, who was now fully conscious and constantly asking for her child. The excuse that she was sleeping was starting to wear thin.

> "Who's feeding her? She needs me for sustenance—"

"She's taken to the bottle. Now, you get some rest."

Julia disappeared, making excuses about a long list of errands still to do.

It was early evening when Shady summoned Julia to the library. Colin was nowhere to be seen.

"No need to be afraid, Julia. He has gone to a union meeting. He won't be home for some time yet."

"I believe that Anna's child has disappeared," said Shady.

Julia nodded in reply.

"I am speaking to you as a confidant," Shady told Julia, "And I don't want a word of this repeated to anyone, not even your friends."

"I am busy ending my relationship with Mr Wheeler," said Shady. "I find him to be a brute. I don't tolerate this type of man in my business relationships, let alone my personal ones. I have known him for many years, and he has always been a charming man. But since he established this new union, well, the power has gone to his head. I am not a cold-hearted woman, and I feel very sorry for young Anna. I have helped many a girl in trouble as best I can. The disappearance of her child affected me very much. I will be putting people out on the street to find little Elizabeth. I don't believe she could kill her own child for one minute. It makes a lot more sense for a mother to orphan a baseborn child than to kill. And several accounts have filtered through of a baby being left on the bridge. I assure you that in a very short while, Anna will have her daughter in her arms."

Julia couldn't believe what she was hearing. She could never have guessed that Shady would come to Anna's aid.

"If you can keep young Anna distracted in the meantime, we will be successful."

"Thank you. Oh, thank you, we had no idea where to begin searching, and Mr Wheeler threatened us with our lives if we said anything to anybody or even make enquiries. We are forbidden to leave the house. He arranged for all the food to be delivered. We can't go anywhere."

"I know," said Shady, "I heard the conversation. But, unlike you, I know quite a lot about him, things he wouldn't want others to know about—and I assure you he will never ever cross me. He has far too much to lose."

Julia went back to Anna and stood over her.

"Elizabeth," rasped Anna.

> "I know, luvvy. Elizabeth is a little angel. I will bring her to you in a few days. I have spoken to the doctor. We must ensure that you are well enough and that the dirty water you swallowed has not made you ill. You are going to see her one of these days—we just can't risk her getting sick. You are getting stronger, and soon, you will be out of danger. Don't worry, Anna, you will have that beautiful little child in your arms again. She's a happy little thing. We're taking good care of her."

Anna nodded and smiled, reassured that Julia was caring for her precious daughter. For the first time in days, she felt better in her own skin. Julia looked down at her friend and hoped to God that Shady would find the child as soon as possible. The thought of telling Anna her child was gone was soul-crushing. The tot wouldn't be the first child to be sold to a baby farm for a few pence. All she could hope for was that someone in the vast crowd could give them information on where Elizabeth disappeared to.

Martha Havelock knocked on the front door of Colin Wheeler house. Sally opened the door and looked at the ragged woman, and smiled. Something in her bones told her the unexpected visitor knew something about Elizabeth.

> "I don't want to get you into trouble, Missus. Come to the servant's entrance, we can talk there. The master is a fierce man."

"I've not come to talk to you. This is urgent business, my dear," answered Miss Hancock, "I have some news for Mr Wheeler I wish to deliver personally."

Sally was motionless.

"Mr Wheeler, are you there?" called the insistent woman. "Oh, Mr Wheeler, I have news for you."

Panicked, Sally let the woman in before anyone spotted the grubby woman yelling on the doorstep.

"Very well then, Miss. Please wait while I fetch the master."

Colin Wheeler went to the parlour and looked at the woman mockingly, pleased she was standing and not dirtying his lovely French furniture.

"Yes?" he asked her. "What can I do for you?"

He looked her up and down as if he had never seen someone from Salford before. As time went on and the subscriptions rolled in, Colin had forgotten his humble roots.

"Mr Wheeler, I've got news for you," said Martha Havelock, excited. "The day that your wife jumped from the Salford bridge, I rescued a baby. And I took it to the poorhouse. Well, not straight away. There was a note with her saying she was to go to Mrs

Wheeler's sister. Only she didn't want her. Anyway, I didn't know that the child was your daughter, and I didn't know its name. So, I left it with the mistress of Prestwick Workhouse. If you want to go and fetch your daughter, Sir, I suggest you speak to the matron."

Colin Wheeler froze, hoping the forced smile looked convincing. This was the last news that he wanted or expected to hear. The longer the child was missing, the more he delighted in presuming its body was festering in the river. He had no intention of ever having that thing in his life again. If and when something happened to Anna, he couldn't put his child out on the street. The public would construe it as abandonment and abuse. If he kept it, he would have to look after it for the rest of his life. He would have to sacrifice money, freedom, and a comfortable life with Shady. He had no intention of doing any of these. He went into his full defensive mode.

"How dare you come to my house and discuss this with me? I don't believe you for one minute. Firstly, you are after money, and you're not getting it from me. Secondly, the child is dead. A boatman found it in the river and took it to the coroner."

"But that's not the story, Sir," objected Martha. "I promise you that I rescued the child. There was a note, and it said that the child's name was Elizabeth. They had a lot of Elizabeth's, so the mistress called her Ellie."

"Where is the note?" Colin asked, fearful that she would produce the evidence.

"I don't have it anymore. The sister took it."

Colin shook his head and looked at her dismissively as if she belonged in an asylum.

"Well, there you go then. You are just another ragamuffin trying to make something out of the situation. Scores of people have already been round saying they know where the baby is," he lied. "Be careful, Miss Hancock. I am a very powerful man, and if you make one more utterance that this abandoned child is mine and you may have a visit from some of my friends in the middle of the night. I am sure that they will use you up until you can't walk."

Martha looked at him, terrified. She had really hoped that her good news would be uplifting, but it had all worked against her. Instead of the revelation leading to a celebration, it turned into a horrible threat. She turned to leave.

"If she was left at the workhouse, what was the surname? Was it mine?" shouted Wheeler.

Martha kept walking and ignored him. Colin ran up behind her and grabbed her arm.

"Don't ignore me when I ask you something," he growled at her.

Martha tried to wrestle out of his grip, and he squeezed until she yelped. She knew he would hurt her if she didn't tell him.

"Ellie. Ellie Prestwich."

Young Sally stood in the shadows. She couldn't see her master or Miss Hancock, but she did hear the child's name.

Colin was restless. Shady lay next to him. He turned over and checked. She was sound asleep. Good. He relived the past few days in his mind. He kept returning to the picture of Anna being carried up the stairs naked, vulnerable, and humiliated. He got out of bed quietly and went to the room where Anna was sleeping. Julia was with her, dozing in a chair in the corner. Colin shook her awake.

"You can go back to your room. I will look after her for the night."

Julia didn't trust him. He leaned in towards her with menace.

"Not to worry, Sir. You get a good night's rest. You're a busy man."

"I said get out," Colin snapped in front of her face.

Julia had no choice but to leave. Instead of going back to her room, she hid in the shadows of a small annexe by the stairs and keenly watched Anna's door like a soldier on sentry duty.

Colin looked down at Anna. She must have sensed someone looming over her, and she opened her eyes.

"You, stupid cow," he muttered.

Anna felt as though she was in a nightmare. She pushed her body into a sitting position.

Colin heard the door open and light footsteps behind him.

"Leave the girl alone, Colin," cautioned a voice.

He turned around to see Shady. Colin wasn't sure what she meant, but by the way she said it, it didn't seem prudent to disobey her command.

Sally gave the details of Miss Hancock's visit to Julia, who wrote the baby's name on a piece of paper. She slipped it to Shady when she served her tea. She didn't say anything. Instead, she simply read the name and nodded.

15

JUSTICE

Martha Havelock felt compelled to go to the authorities. The conversation that she had with Colin Wheeler was disturbing, and she was in fear for her life. She was taking a great risk by reporting his threats to the Peelers because he had many policemen friends, and a corrupt officer would soon tell Wheeler that she had laid a complaint against him. Then what?

Martha arrived at the police station. The weather was foul, and she tended to be superstitious. It was obviously a premonition of her death. So be it. The rotter Wheeler had no right to treat her the way he had. Justice will prevail, she told herself. She was right.

As many friends as Colin Wheeler had bought, so he had enemies. Certain coppers would have put him away without thinking twice, and they had been waiting a long time to have enough evidence to arrest him for his dodgy deals and embezzling of union funds. Someone had to be brave enough to testify against Wheeler. Martha was not that person, but she would certainly be added to the list of plaintiffs. Sat on a chair in the station, she waited for a constable to take her statement.

She heard a great noise behind her, and she turned around and watched two detectives escorting Jimmy Blackbeard to the cells. A burly young man, he was well known as one of the most violent thugs that Angel Meadows had to offer. Blackbeard was shouting at the top of their lungs and telling the officers to let him go.

> "I promise you, guv," he shouted loudly, "I know nothing about it. I've got nothing to do with it."
>
> "Stop lying to us Jimmy, we have two witnesses who saw the woman pass you the money. Not everybody is as loyal as you think they are."

These words enraged the rogue. He was convinced that he was a mighty man in the criminal underworld of Manchester. In fact, Jimmy was just another thug who had been allowed to roam the streets for far too long. The police had always suspected him of being responsible for the deaths of two young boys he bullied and finally murdered for not taking orders from him. Now, he was in a different situation. The police had two witnesses who swore that they had seen Jimmy being paid by a woman to stab Dickie Woods to death. The police knew that Jimmy was the murderer, and now they were looking for the paymaster.

"Look, squire—"

"Sir, to you, Jimmy," Detective Bragg reprimanded.

"—Sir—I've never stabbed anyone, you know that. We might be involved in a little bit of petty theft from time to time, us boys don't go around stabbing people for money. We don't rub people out. We ain't never done that before."

Constable Ashley had been a policeman for twelve years, and he was a seasoned officer. He had walked his beat in most of Salford and Angel Meadows and was familiar with all the criminal operations. Every street had a gang of Scuttlers, a vicious lot of youngsters who showed no mercy for their victims. Ashley ignored Jimmy Blackbeard's protestations and pushed him into his cell. He would have to wait until the detectives had a go at him, and they were determined to extract as much information as they could."

The constable returned to his desk and smiled at Martha

"Right-o, Miss—er?"

"Havelock."

"How can I help you today?"

"Well, it goes like this," began Martha. "You know that the young woman who threw herself off the bridge is Colin Wheeler wife. She had a little baby with her. While everybody was watching the mess unfold under the bridge, I picked up the baby. There was a note on the child. I thought that the mother was dead, so I picked up the little thing. There was a letter tucked in the blanket, and I took the baby to the address on the note. I had to get her out of the cold and to safety. The next day, I heard the talk of the street the woman was Mr Wheeler's wife."

Constable Ashley smiled at her.

"You did a very brave thing. You probably saved that child's life. I truly commend you for the responsibility that you showed taking the baby to safety."

"Well, constable, this is where it becomes tricky," said Martha. "Let me tell you everything that happened after that."

The constable listened carefully and wrote down everything. He couldn't believe that two family members had turned away the child, especially Colin Wheeler, the father.

"This is all very confusing," said Constable Ashley.

"That's what I am telling you, constable. I sense the mother is still alive and probably right inside that house of Mr Wheeler. He took her there after she was rescued. There is something fishy about it all. When I went round, none of the clocks were stopped or anything like that. She's alive, I tell ya."

"We will investigate your report immediately, Miss Havelock. What is the name of the woman you called on?"

"I don't know. I can't read. But I can take you to her home. She is a very posh lady who lives nearby in one of those large mansions."

"So, she doesn't live here in Salford or The Meadows?" asked Constable Ashley.

"No. Miserable sod she was. I was only trying to do right by the bairn. I don't want their bleedin' money. She looked down her nose at me as if I was a tramp."

"I am sorry about that," said the constable.

Martha explained how she took the child to the Prestwich Workhouse.

"I left her in the care of a very kind mistress," said Martha.

"Yes?"

"Yes," answered Martha, "but they gave her a new name because they didn't know what her surname was, and they were full to the rafters with Elizabeths apparently."

"Which was?"

"Ellie Prestwich, after the workhouse."

Jimmy Blackbeard was kicking up such a fuss in the cells that it took two policemen to return him after questioning. Bragg followed alongside. Acting incensed, he shouted out his innocence in front of the whole police station. For a moment, Constable Ashley thought that Jimmy's life was wasted on crime. He would have excelled as a thespian. It was clearly a ruse, so he didn't get his throat slit for being a grass. Detective Bragg was tired of getting stonewalled by the gangs and wanted a conviction, and he was going to get one.

"I do apologies for the disturbance, Miss Havelock."

The poor girl gave a nervous smile, wondering if Jimmy was one of Wheeler's henchmen.

"Stop all your bloody ranting, Jimmy. We have evidence that you took the money. Witnesses to say that you stabbed Dickie Woods to death. After that, you hit the town with a lot of cash on the hip. You spent a fortune on girls and went on an all-night bender. Now you know that even for a petty criminal, this is a lot of money to spend all at once."

"Ah, but my mum gave it to me. She is so good to me," said Jimmy, tears welling in his eyes.

Constable Ashley shook his head in wonderment.

"Jimmy, your mum has been dead for seven years now, lad. We all know that."

Jimmy couldn't think of any more lies to tell. His creativity was depleted. Finally, despondency took hold of him. This is exactly what the detectives were waiting for.

"You must understand, Jimmy, you are going to hang for this crime. I don't believe that there is any hope for you."

Jimmy tried to look nonchalant, but his mouth was quivering, and his eyes were darting all over the room.

"All we want to know is who gave you the money to kill Dicky Woods."

Jimmy shook his head.

"It may cause the judge to be more lenient toward you if you cooperate with us."

Jimmy sat up straight in the chair for the first time since his arrest. He realised the gravity of the situation. The idea of hanging from his neck until he was dead held no appeal. The Peelers were right. Why should he take all the blame for Dickie Woods death?

"Right, you have me there," said Blackbeard. "If I tell you everything, can you save my life? Will the court show me mercy?"

"We can't speak for the judge. We can only ask him on the day. There have been cases where he has shown mercy. To be honest, you may not hang, but you will spend the rest of your life a guest of Her Majesty."

Jimmy was terrified. The idea of going to the gallows, walking up the wooden steps having the noose put over his head in front of a jeering crowd was horrific. A select few would watch, delighted that there would be one less criminal on the streets. The thoughts filled him with a fear he had never experienced before. He knew that his life in gaol would hold no comfort, but he would get used to it. Maybe even bump into a few old pals who had already had their collars felt. However, the imminent threat of the noose snapping his neck felt far more terrifying than a confined space.

"The other lads didn't see her face, Jimmy. Making excuses, it was dark. But you know who it is, don't you? So, come on, lad, out with it."

Jimmy looked down at the desk, weighing up the pros and cons of his future. It was bleak.

> "It was that horrible hook-nosed harpy, Mary Errington," said Jimmy. "She put a hundred quid in my hand. I couldn't believe what I was seeing. I swear the only reason she didn't do it herself was that she could have got blood on that fancy dress she was wearing. You know that one. Funny old bird she is. Always wanting to live way higher than her station. She comes from the bleedin' Meadows. I don't know where she got the money from, but she handed it over without flinching. I had got the feeling that she had a lot more. I was bloody stupid. I should have robbed her of everything she had instead of killing Dicky Woods."

This was all the detectives were waiting to hear. They grabbed Jimmy by the scruff of his neck again and pulled him out of the seat. This time the tearaway was more compliant. He had talked himself into a corner. He couldn't retract his statement. He had confessed to the murder of Dicky Woods and revealed the paymaster.

Two detective constables arrived outside of Mary Riddle's apartment at the same moment as Constable Ashley and Martha Havelock.

> "What are you doing here, constable?" asked Detective Bragg.

"We are looking for a missing baby, Sir," he answered.

"We are looking for a more sinister character," said Bragg. "We're going to arrest a woman called Mary Errington. Married to a prominent solicitor, a Mr Alec Riddle.

"I remember him quite well from when I walked the beat in Salford." gasped the constable. "Had a small law firm down Churchill Road, I believe. What a pity this woman is his wife. He seemed quite an honourable fellow. This scandal will drag him down. We don't really know who we are looking for," smiled Constable Ashley. "I am relying on Martha here to take me to the door of someone who might have information about the child. We know where it is, and we are trying to reunite it with its mother, or at least its blood family."

The excitement was too much for Martha, and she couldn't keep quiet any longer.

"Yes, Sir. We are off to find a woman on the second floor, the aunt," said Martha, who promptly began to tell the detectives the entire story of little Elizabeth as they all trudged up the stairs. The two detectives looked at each other without saying anything. Then, when they could finally squeeze a word in, they added:

"Will show us the way, Miss Havelock. I believe that we are looking for the same person."

Martha led them up to the second-floor landing, delighting in the idea of the officers arresting the horrible woman who had threatened to call the police on her. It was deliciously ironic that the shoe was on the other foot. Martha felt so empowered with the police alongside her. Not only was this woman a heartless creature, but possibly a murderer.

She gave the door knocker three loud bangs. The door was opened by a distinguished gentleman.

"Good day, officers," he said with a smile. "How can I be of assistance?"

"Sir, we are looking for a Miss Mary Errington."

"That will be my wife. She is no longer Miss Errington—she's now Mrs Riddle."

A woman came up behind him, looking hard-faced and distinctly predatory. She looked from Martha to the officers, annoyed the wretched smelly woman had brought the police back to her house because she didn't want to take in her sister's brat.

"That's her!" shouted Martha, pointing straight ahead. "That baby is in an orphanage because of you, you horrible woman."

"How can I help you?" Mary asked politely. "I am too busy to listen to that woman's ranting. She's already annoyed me once this week, and I will have her arrested if she harasses me any further."

"You and Mr Wheeler have both turned the baby away," protested Martha. "I want to find the child's mother. You don't have a heart, do you?"

"The child is nothing to me," Mary said coolly. "Mr Wheeler is not her father. She is the illegitimate child of my sister Anna. She had pre-marital relations with Mr Mario Perreira and fell pregnant. I don't know where Anna is, and I don't care. She deserves her lot."

Alec Riddle turned to look at her in dismay.

"I will never look after my sister's baseborn child. She can rot in an orphanage."

It was the final blow for Alec Riddle. Most families looked after each other. Without a doubt, he had made a terrible mistake by marrying this cruel monster. He remembered how much he had cared for her and taken her away from her horrible life in Angel Meadows. He also remembered the money he pushed into her hand every time she visited him. Helped her become independent. Now it dawned on him, Mary had prostituted herself to manipulate him for her own ends, and that was all there was to their sorry little relationship. A relationship that would soon be over. Mary was still busy quoting the law to the policemen when Alec Riddle interrupted her.

"Be quiet, Mary," said Alec, "Let the detective speak."

Bragg stepped forward and looked into Mary's eyes.

"Mrs Riddle, you are under arrest for the murder of Dickie Woods."

16

HELP FROM AN UNEXPECTED SOURCE

Shady had made many powerful friends through her discrete establishment. One such friend was Lord Somerset. Shady's operation was unique because it had no name and did not represent the typical red-brocade monstrosities that catered for a more sordid following. Instead, her clientele was a collection of high-ranking politicians, wealthy business owners and young aristocrats sowing their wild oats. It was to one of the politicians that she turned to in her for help.

Shady sent a message to Lord Somerset's Manchester office, telling him that she would like to meet with him that evening. The invitation surprised him. It wasn't often that he was asked to visit Shady. Usually, he was the one calling for her services.

Shady picked him for more than his power Lord Somerset was a cheerful fellow and was always in good spirits. He was easy to get along with and treated the women that he went with very well. He had never been barred, and he didn't drink himself into a stupor.

Lord Somerset's story was very sad. He had fallen in love with his wife at a young age. They were best of friends and lovers. He had taken her on honeymoon to the south of France, along the Camargue. On a splendid Sunday afternoon, they chose to go horse riding on the beach. She was pitched off the wild stallion she rode and broke her back. Although disabled, Lord Somerset dedicated his life to her. He had tried to make love to his wife after the accident but numbed from the waist down, she couldn't respond as she used to. Every attempt at intimacy had him feeling as if he was violating her. Lord Somerset had met Shady after the opera one night. He had poured his heart out to her, and she had invited him to the business to help him resolve his little domestic issue.

There was a gentle knock at the door, and Shady swung it open.

"Hello, my dear," said Lord Somerset with a smile.

"Hello, Thomas. You are looking well."

"It is not often that I get summoned here with such urgency. Can I be of assistance? I have developed an excellent reputation as a fine lover," he added with a chuckle.

Shady laughed, the man was pleasant to interact with, and she felt empathy for his situation. She always instructed her girls to be kind and warned them against any tendency to exploit him. He was one of the people that Shady would protect no matter what.

Shady gave him a playful punch on the chest.

"You!"

"Ah, it is always a pleasure to visit you, Shady, my dear. Even if I am only destined to have a cup of tea and a chat."

"Take a seat, Thomas. I have a little problem."

She poured out a cup of Darjeeling and passed it over to him.

"Are you still a board member of the Prestwich Workhouse Committee?" she asked

"Yes, I am. It is time that hole had some new blood injected into it. It is rotten from top to bottom. I mean it. The board members are ineffective. The staff are miserable. The building is rotting."

Shady took a seat opposite and a sip of her drink.

"Of course, I am not one of the most popular people on the committee. Or the richest. Or the most influential. Nobody listens to a word I tell them," he chuckled quietly.

"Thomas, I am looking for a child. I don't know if she is at the Prestwich Workhouse or the orphanage, but I need the child to be brought to me. I know the mother, and I want the two reconciled."

"And the father?" asked Lord Somerset.

"That's a very complicated situation. The girl was young and inexperienced. Ended up in the family way. The father cast her off. She's now married to a very powerful man who would like her separated from her daughter. He is not in love with her, and since he is not the father, he now wants nothing to do with the child, after—erm—"

"Who is this person?"

"I would prefer not to say. He is a client, and you know I pride myself on my discretion. I have learnt of this sorry story through his staff."

"You know that I can't steal a child from the workhouse."

"Of course, I understand, but this is a unique situation. The young woman tried to take her life to give the child a better start in life as an orphan. It's so sad."

"I can't make any promises, Shady, but I will do my best. Does the child have a name?"

"Yes, they gave her one when she was admitted," said Shady with a smile, protecting her source. "Ellie Prestwich."

17

MISSING

Fog draped everything in a white shroud. Andrew Keegan was surprised that the ferry was allowed to dock in the Liverpool harbour, certain that all the other ships would have to lie outside the harbour until the cloud lifted.

The Irishman had a simple portmanteau with him, not wanting to bog himself down with luggage. He found his way to the railway station and waited for the next train to Manchester. The train squealed, rattled, and puffed its way from the station and into the countryside. It wasn't far to Manchester, and soon he could see a dark cloud looming in the distance as he approached the heartland of manufacturing in Lancashire.

The city was dark and grotty. Nothing had any charm, not even the people. When they heard his Irish accent, they became belligerent. The population had suffered the influx of the desperate Irish for decades. The common people had little sympathy for their plight and were unaccepting of the poor wretches, their only crime being desperate to survive. All the locals experienced was the Irish gobbling up their food, poaching their jobs and overcrowding the rows.

Andrew Keegan found a room above a small pub. The establishment proudly advertised comfort, but when he finally got to his room, it was furnished only with a rickety bed, a cracked chamber pot and a stained enamel washbasin. The blanket was threadbare. The only welcome came from a small potbelly stove in the corner. Andrew was prepared to tolerate all the discomfort. Every second of hardship was worth it if he could find Anna and Elizabeth. He had no idea where he would begin to look. He toyed with visiting the police, but he didn't have much faith that they would have the information he was looking for. He worried he might make things more difficult for Anna—if she were still alive. But he had to start somewhere. He took heart that there had not been an obituary in the paper at least.

Anna was beginning to feel better as her bedrest continued. She found it easier to sit up, and she could even drink hot beverages without tears of pain coming to her eyes. However, one thing bothered her—Elizabeth's absence. Whilst she accepted Julia's advice that it was too risky for her daughter to be in close proximity, she had not heard so much as a child's squeal permeating the quiet house. The longer it went on, the more she was certain something was amiss.

She didn't want to be under Colin's roof, feeling very unsafe ever since she had awoken with him looming over her. Anna had heard Shady calling him out of the room, which convinced her if her brute of a husband was allowed to stay, he would have violated her. Of course, she was still his wife, and he was still entitled to his conjugal rights, but she didn't want to provide them, especially if he was already being satisfied by painted ladies.

It was all very confusing. The woman invited by her husband into their marital bed had also saved her from the pain of being forcibly taken. Anna didn't know if Shady was truly aware of Wheeler's intentions. If she was, the young woman was grateful for her intervention.

Julia, Sally and Cook, however cheerful, couldn't raise Anna out of her despair. She expected they have some chit-chat about the baby sooner or later, but there was nothing. Finally, when Julia brought in some tea, Anna decided to confront her.

> "I know that Elizabeth is not in this house. I can feel it. Where has Colin sent her?"

Julia couldn't meet Anna's eyes.

"Tell me now," Anna demanded. "I need to know."

Julia shook her head.

"Oh no! Don't tell me they've taken the child from me for her own protection because I am such a bad mother. Please don't tell me that!" screamed Anna frantically, her throat feeling like dry parchment and burning like fire.

"No. No. I have got it now. He has secretly given her away to another family. He made no bones about not wanting her. Why would he? She's so dark-skinned. Everyone will know he's not the father. The thought of another childless family raising my beloved girl! Oh, God, what have I done."

Julia looked up, tears in her eyes.

"Stop it, Anna, stop it. You're right that she's not her, but you're wrong about everything else. Our best hope Shady. She has the most influence, and if anybody can find Elizabeth, she can. A woman called round saying she picked her up the night you—"

"What was I thinking when I left her alone on that bridge. I trusted my sister Mary to care for her. I thought she would have a better life without me. Why, why, was I so stupid? Of course, she would turn Elizabeth away."

Julia took Anna's hand as the tears streamed down her face. Anna couldn't take much more. The housekeeper had never seen a human in such despair.

Anna pushed Julia away from her. She lifted the blankets and slid her legs onto the floor. As she stood up, she felt dizzy, and the room spun around her. She clutched at the bedframe.

> "What are you doing, Anna? You'll do yourself a mischief, girl!"
>
> "I have to find Elizabeth before Mary gives her away," rasped Anna
>
> "You are in no condition to get up."

Anna ignored her warning. She managed to progress halfway across the room, and everything went black in front of her eyes. As she fainted, Julia rushed to help her. Anna collapsed into Julia's arms and lost consciousness.

> "Besides, it's too late, petal. That sister of yours didn't want her," Julia choked.

*

Outside, Mario watched Colin walk out of his front door. Usually, Colin took a cab directly to the dockside offices, but on Thursdays, he would leave his home in the morning, take a stroll to buy a newspaper, and then go to his favourite barber. It was a nice little ritual he relished. As Colin reached the newsagents, Mario grabbed him by the elbow and shoved him into a narrow lane.

"What the hell do you want?" demanded Colin pompously.

"My daughter," said Mario.

"So, now she is your daughter?" Colin mocked.

"I am looking for Anna. The baby is missing, and I want to find my child."

"Well bugger off you spoilt little runt, or I will send somebody to take care of you."

Mario's heart began to beat faster. His vendetta with Colin Wheeler had more resting on it than finding his daughter. He had always longed for a good reason to confront Colin, a man who assumed he won the upper hand when he won Anna's hand in marriage. Now her former lover had the perfect opportunity.

"Tell me where to find her," insisted Mario.

"I don't know where she is. Her mother gave her away, remember. Or she drowned in the river. It matters not."

"Stop lying. You know more than that. Tell me, or I will kill you."

"You aren't a man enough to kill me. You weren't even man enough to hold onto Anna or your own child. You're a stupid mummy's boy. So do me a favour and go back to Mama."

Mario lost control. This man had humiliated him so many times, and he couldn't allow it to continue. Mario put his hand in his pocket and ran his fingers along the edge of a switchblade knife.

"Come on, then, Mario, lad. Do you think you can take on a big man like me?"

Colin started to laugh loudly. He spread out his arms, exposing his chest, goading Mario land a punch. The young man saw his opportunity, rushed forward, arm in the air, and plunged the knife through his foe's ribs and into his heart.

Colin collapsed onto the gravel path, blood seeping into his mouth. Mario put his foot on Colin's head and pushed it into the stones.

"The name, big man. Give me the name of the child."

Blood bubbled out of Colin's mouth. Mario got down next to him. Dazed, Wheeler was rapidly losing consciousness. Mario was lucky. It was one of those rare occasions when the belligerent union man capitulated.

"Ellie—," he gasped. "—Ellie Prestwich."

Those were Colin's last words as his body relaxed and slumped. Then, finally, the twinkling light in

Colin's roguish eyes was extinguished. All that was left was a vacant mocking stare.

A young governess was on her way to lessons when she passed the alley. She recognised Mario from the greengrocer's shop. Filled with terror, she found a bobby walking the beat and took him back to the alley. Constable Ashley ran behind the hysterical young woman. She refused to go into the lane and just pointed. He shook his head when he saw the corpse. *'Well, well, well. If it isn't Colin Wheeler.'*

18

THE GUILTY AND THE INNOCENT

Andrew Keegan was by far the most handsome man that Julia had ever seen. As soon as she saw him on the front step, she was smitten. The tall, handsome Irishman didn't smile, but he was polite.

"Is this the home of Mr Colin Wheeler?" he asked Julia.

"Yes, Sir. But he isn't at home."

"I see."

Andrew sounded frustrated.

"Have you a business appointment to see him, Sir?"

"No, it is a personal matter."

"May I give him a message?" the housekeeper enquired.

"Yes, please. Tell him I am looking for Anna Wheeler. That is if she survived—"

Julia's face must have given her away.

"Where is she?" Andrew asked gently.

"I don't know," answered Julia.

"I think you do. She stayed in Ireland to have a child," said Andrew, "Where are they? I just know she's not dead."

"Sir, I am going to lose my job if I speak to you," Julia said furtively as she looked to check Colin was not eavesdropping. "Mr Wheeler is—"

"I know all about the sort of man Colin is," Andrew consoled. "I am not surprised Anna fled like she did."

It was clear the visitor had empathy for Julia and a deep love for Anna.

"Just give me a name. If you don't let me see Anna, I have to find that child for her."

Julia nodded.

"If you want to help, go and see a lady called Hawkins."

Julia gave him the address. She was in two minds to tell him that Anna was in the house but decided against it. She knew that Shady Hawkins was a sophisticated woman, and she would get a good measure of the man.

*

Mary Errington Riddle stood before the judge. The case was cut and dried. She had instructed the murder of Dicky Woods. The judge saw fit to try her immediately, as Mary had signed a confession and admitted her guilt. Mary believed that she was being noble, admitting her crime. Irrespective of the rule of law, thinking back to the stunts he had pulled to swindle her father out of the family's money and the long adulterous relationship with her feckless mother, Mary believed that she had done the right thing. Dicky Woods was no more than a maggot, and she was glad that he was dead.

Alec Riddle didn't attend the trial. Instead, he spent the morning finalising his work and packing his clothes. His relationship with Mary had cost him dearly. He would never be able to practise the law again. It was his own fault. He had embarked on a relationship with a very young girl, and he would never forgive himself for his stupidity. Alec thought that he was giving Mary the prospect of a good life and an education. Little did he know that if he had not been the fool to fall for her, it would have been someone else she sunk her talons into.

Alec wanted to get as far away from Manchester as possible, to begin a new life, possibly as a teacher. He sent Miss Jenkins to book him a berth on a ship to Australia.

"There is a ship leaving for Sydney tonight, Sir," she said.

"Thank you. That is perfect."

"Will you be coming back, Sir?"

"No, Miss Jenkins, I will never return to England."

*

There was no name on the beautiful house. It could have belonged to any wealthy man in Manchester, but it didn't. It was the residence of a woman. Andrew was impressed. The house had a hugely impressive Georgian-style frontage, painted in pristine white. The garden was immaculate. When he walked through the gate, a friendly gardener greeted him.

"Are you looking for the lady of the house, Sir?"

"Yes, Mrs Hawkins."

"Miss Hawkins," the gardener corrected him.

Andrew smiled.

"There is a bell next to the door. Just give it two tugs. Only two."

Andrew tugged the chord twice, and finally, the door was opened by a beautiful young woman.

"Good afternoon," he greeted kindly, "I am here to see Miss Hawkins."

"Is it serious business, Sir?"

Andrew was puzzled by the strange question.

"Err—yes, I happen to think so, Miss."

"Follow with me," the beauty instructed politely.

As Andrew was led through the house, he began to realise what business Miss Hawkins ran. A bevy of lovely ladies were scattered about the house. Some were reading, others chattering in little groups. Each woman was breathtakingly beautiful and fully dressed.

Andrew was shown into Shady's study. It was a stately affair, fit for a king. Little did he know that her most prominent client was only one rank lower than the queen's consort.

Shady walked toward Andrew and put out her hand.

"Welcome to my home," she greeted with a smile.

"Thank you."

"Can I pour you something to drink?"

"Yes, please. Scotch if you have it."

"Have you been referred to my business by anybody in particular?" asked Shady.

"Yes, Miss Hawkins, a young maid who works in the home of Colin Wheeler has sent me here."

Shady cocked her head to one side and seemed confused.

"Miss Hawkins, I am looking for a young woman, Anna Wheeler, Mr Wheeler's wife."

"And what is your interest in Mrs Wheeler?" asked Shady.

"May I speak freely?"

"Of course, we protect many secrets in this house."

"I am in love with her. I met her on a ferry to Ireland. She was pregnant and the most beautiful woman I had ever seen. She was full of joy. She delighted in everything. Then I read about her in the newspaper. Something terrible must have happened for her to want to take her life. I want to find her. Save her from Colin."

Shady was a hopeless romantic at heart, and the story intrigued her.

"I watched her give birth to her daughter, I was heartbroken to watch her leave Dublin, but she was dedicated to her husband, no matter how flawed the fellow is."

"Yes, he is a terrible man. I might as well tell you. If you ask around in the right places, you will learn that I was in an affair with him after he married Anna."

Andrew looked at her in shock. Was she the reason why Anna had tried to take her life? Why would she want to help? Clearly, the woman wasn't to be trusted.

"Mr Keegan, I have contacted somebody who may be able to get the child back to us. It has been quite a trial to track her down. I trust this person. Anna is at Mr Wheeler's house. She is still very sick from her ordeal. Young Julia tells me that she is suffering terrible despair."

"Colin Wheeler will never let me see her," said Andrew.

"Earlier, I received a note from a client who also happens to be a policeman. Mr Wheeler is dead. Just after nine o'clock this morning, he was found stabbed to death in a lane near his house. Mr Wheeler will no longer be a problem."

All his exhaustion left him from the sleepless night in his squalid little room left him. Even though he had been taught otherwise in church, he was delighted to hear of another man's death, a man he had never even met. The ogre was out of Anna's life.

*

For a second time that day, Andrew Keegan knocked on the Wheeler's door.

"I know she is here," he said firmly. "Can I see her, please?"

Julia nodded but denied his request.

"Sir, she has gone to the Belle Vue Prison, Gorton, to visit her sister. She is too sick to make the trip, but she wouldn't listen. She was summoned by the superintendent at the gaol. Her sister wanted to see her."

Andrew sank onto the steps. Everything was a riddle and a nightmare at the same time. He was being sent from pillar to post, and it felt that Anna was eluding him.

"I tell you what. Why don't you come in? I will make you tea, and you can wait for Anna. On one condition. When she gets back, you must give her time to settle and rest. The poor thing is exhausted. I don't want you rushing in like a bull in a China shop upsetting her. It will be quite a strain you turning up out of the blue like this."

"Thank you," he said with a sigh, open to agreeing to anything if it meant he got to see his beloved Anna again.

He hoped she still felt the same way about him. Was she even the same person he met in Dublin? That girl wouldn't have jumped in the river.

*

The bright sun shone down on the buttery-coloured prison building, making it seem more cheerful than it was. Young Sally and the cab driver helped Anna out of the coach and escorted her to the visitors' entrance. She was shown to the superintendent's office.

"You seem very fragile. Mrs Wheeler, perhaps you must cancel the interview with your sister. What you hear may not be good for your health."

"I will see her," rasped Anna. "Why is she here?"

"Murder. She will be executed at sunset tonight. Quarter to eight, I believe,"

A warden led Anna to a cell separate from the rest of the gaol, and she sat down on an old wooden chair. A short while later, they arrived with Mary. Her sister had shackles on her wrists and ankles. Anna burst into tears when she saw her.

"Oh, Mary," she cried, "it can't be true. They have made a mistake. Can your husband help you?"

"Stop snivelling. It's no time to be sentimental. I had Dicky Woods killed, and I would do it again."

"Oh, Mary! Why did you do that? Were you protecting us? Did you tell the judge that you were protecting us?" cried Anna.

Mary began to snort an awkward attempt at some sort of laugh. Her eyes were wild, and her face was evil.

"Protecting us? You stupid girl."

Anna had no idea what Mary was leaning towards.

"I am Dicky Woods' daughter."

"But so am I, Mary. I didn't feel the need to murder him."

"No, Anna," said Mary in a quiet voice. "I lied. You are Bernard's daughter."

"But you wrote a letter telling me that Dicky Woods was my father. I believed you."

"It's quite simple. I wanted you to feel as much self-disgust as I did. I hated the greedy little man. And seeing him bed our mother in front of us, well, that was the last straw. He deserved it."

"And Elizabeth. Did anybody take Elizabeth to your house? I don't know where she is."

"Yes, a ragged woman arrived with the little sod the night you jumped. Told me I had to honour the wishes in the note. I tore that up soon enough. I wasn't interested in the thing. I told her to get it the poorhouse."

Anna couldn't believe what she was hearing. In a short space of time, her sister had become even more of a stranger. Anna was furious. If she had more energy, she would have beaten Mary to a pulp.

"Which poorhouse? There are three!"

"I don't know, and I don't care."

Mary's cold beady eyes flitted across her sister's face, which infuriated Anna. Why was she always so distant? Calculating?

"I had come here to console you. But you don't deserve my help. You deserve to die," spat Anna.

"Perhaps I've always been dead," Mary lamented.

Anna got up and banged against the door with the palm of her hand.

"Get me out of here," she bellowed until she was freed.

"Are you sure you don't want to spend the last hours with her sister?"

"Definitely not," Anna grizzled. "I can be of no comfort to her. She is a monster."

Sally looked at Anna, who was thunderous all the way home.

*

It was late in the afternoon by the time they returned. The house was well-lit and welcoming. As Sally escorted Anna into the kitchen, she had a strange sense that everything felt lighter. The staff were on tenterhooks. It was clear Anna knew nothing of her husband's demise. Their eyes met behind her back as they silently negotiated who would tell their mistress she was a widow. No one dared mention Andrew Keegan waiting in the parlour.

The house was warm, and everyone was dashing about. She picked up on no one wanting to sit with her, not even for a moment, and she felt very alone. She looked out of the window, keeping an eye on the sun as it sank down in the smoggy air.

It had been one of the worst days of her life. Her sister Mary, facing the last hour of her life, had lied to her about her parentage. That lie had set in motion a series of events that had destroyed everyone in her family.

Sat slumped in the kitchen, it was left to Julia to break the news that Colin Wheeler had been murdered, stabbed to death by an as yet unknown assassin.

But that mattered not. The most pressing matter remained. The poor mother didn't know where her precious Elizabeth was. She gazed blankly, trying to work out which workhouse of the three to check first. Oh, how she wanted to start looking there and then, but there was no way she would be able to speak to someone that late in the day.

"You have visitors, Anna. They are waiting for you in the library," said Cook

Anna anticipated that they were there to pay their respects to her and prepared herself to greet them, then changed her plan. The hallway clock struck a quarter to the hour. Outside, the sun was setting.

"Please give me a few moments," said Anna.

*

Mary climbed the scaffolding and stood on the platform. This wasn't Tyburn or Newgate. Times had changed. There were no bloodthirsty onlookers jeering and shouting insults at her. Mary was just where she wanted to be—facing the end of a tiresome, unfulfilling existence. She didn't feel sorry for herself and gave no thought to her husband nor had any remorse for her actions. As an atheist, she refused the offer of any religious sacraments.

Mary bobbed and weaved as the executioner tried to put the black hood over her head. She wanted the true experience of death through her own eyes. His assistant held her arms still as he ignored her wishes and pulled the hood down further, confident not a shred of light leaked in. The hangman pulled out his pocket watch and checked it. Seven forty-five. It was officially sunset.

There was no countdown or warning. The trap door simply opened.

19

THE VISITORS

Anna felt tearful for a moment but composed herself, not wanting to cause a scene in front of the guests. Julia helped her along into the hallway.

"You do look a sight for sore eyes," Julia chuckled as she ruffled her friend's stubbly hair.

Anna reached up to her head and felt her long luscious locks were gone. She could hardly talk, and she walked like an old woman. Her confidence evaporated.

"Who's here?" Anna asked. "If I'm honest, I don't feel like seeing anyone. Please don't let it be some of Colin's wretched union bores. I'm not in the mood."

"You can relax. It is Shady accompanied by a polite young man I have never met before."

Anna thought of Andrew. She would never have left Dublin if she had not been married to Colin. How different the last few days would have been if she'd dared to stay, the nerve to follow her heart.

She stood in the doorway of the library, and her tired eyes bored into Sandy Hawkins, still not knowing if she should trust the woman or not.

"Hello, Anna."

"Shady," answered Anna coolly.

"I have a lot to explain to you."

"Yes, you do."

"You must understand. I never wanted to hurt you. I knew you only married Colin to give your child a father. I was trying to help you by agreeing to him becoming a client. I could see his resentment of the arrangement was beginning to fester. I will make it up to you."

"Never! You can never make it better."

"I promise, I will."

Over in the far corner, it seemed a young man was looking out of the window, back to Anna, holding something in his arms.

"I have brought two very special people to visit you."

Andrew slowly turned around.

"You!" she trilled.

"Yes, I had to find you."

In his arms was a baby, sleeping snugly in a warm blanket. The fabric looked distinctly unfamiliar, nothing like the sheet had wrapped Elizabeth in.

"Who is that?" asked Anna suspiciously.

"Ellie," he answered. "Come and look at her."

"I don't want to see someone else's baby. I want my own child back."

Furious, she stomped over to him.

"How could you deceive me like this? You should know better."

Anna reached Andrew and tried to stand on her toes to get a better look at the child. Could it be? He bent forward and kissed Anna on her forehead. It was the most comforting kiss anyone had ever given her.

"Look at her," Andrew whispered. "I am sure you will love her."

Anna peered into the bundle of blankets and saw the dark curls and olive skin. He allowed her to grab the child out of his arms. The baby shook awake. Little Elizabeth looked up at Anna with big black eyes and began to smile. Anna began to cry.

Andrew put his arms around Anna and cradled both to him.

"Anna, I am taking you and Elizabeth home with me. If you'll let me?"

Andrew kissed Anna the way he would have liked to when they first met on the Liverpool to Dublin ferry.

"Your family? What will they say?"

"Wonderful things. They know that we are in love and to be married. The Keegan clan can't wait to meet my wife and child."

****

THE END

Other books in the Sisters Sagas series

The Sailor's Lost Daughters
With her sister vanishing from the Angel Meadows slum, left unwanted and unloved, orphan Ruby soon knew that no-one was coming looking for her. How would the little girl survive alone.

Buy The Sailor's Lost Daughters

View all Emma's books on Amazon

About the author

I live in London with my husband and two dogs. I love bringing the Victorian world to life and researching true stories to inspire my romance and saga books. I hope I have created a little bit of light escapism for you to enjoy.

Thank you for all your support.

Best wishes,

Emma.

www.emmahardwick.co.uk

Printed in Great Britain
by Amazon

70626688R00161